Short and Strange

Betsy Nelson

ISBN: 1974103668
ISBN-13: 9781974103669

DEDICATION

This collection of stories is dedicated to the memory of Madeleine L'Engle (11/29/1918 to 9/6/2007) who is the author of "The Wrinkle in Time" series. It is because of her work that I know it is possible to love God and enjoy reading fantasy at the same time.

"Maybe you have to know the darkness
before you can appreciate the light." - M. L'Engle

CONTENTS

Preface

Writing stories is a lot like reading, but in slow motion. I have to keep on writing to find out how the story ends. This may make no sense. You may think "Surely she knows – she is writing the story", but this isn't how it is at all.

Stories write themselves – you are just along for the ride. Stories are like babies. You give them a place to be created and you nurture them, but they grow up on their own. They turn out exactly how they are supposed to be – but not always how you expected.

This is what happened here. These stories were inspired by unusual black and white pictures that I found. It is presumed that the images are old enough that they are public domain. All future editions of this book will reflect any changes necessitated by further information.

So what genre are these stories? Fiction, certainly, but what kind? Some might say they are sci-fi, but there isn't any science or fantasy in them. You will not find any robots or dragons – or even robotic dragons - within these pages. Perhaps a better term is "speculative fiction". This is fiction with a twist, where something out of the ordinary happens, something more than you would find in an average fiction piece. Some of the stories are very strange, while some are just odd. Some are almost normal. But what is normal, after all?

I hope you enjoy reading these stories as much as I enjoyed writing them. I had not written fiction until I started this project, and have been pleasantly surprised to see that it isn't as hard as I thought it was. Hopefully you too will be inspired to write something equally as surprising.

-Betsy Nelson

August 8th, 2017

Nashville, TN

Short and Strange

The longest day of Theodore Smythe

Theodore was tired, more tired than he had ever been. This had been the longest day he'd ever known. He wasn't even sure what day it was, or what year. He'd only been alive for three years and two months. That was when Timmy had gotten him for his fifth birthday. Before that, he was just a stuffed doll, a bear. Once he had bonded with his child he became a Bear, a real being. Every year when Timmy's birthday rolled around, Theodore had a birthday too. It was the day he became alive. They even made him his own cake, but smaller. It was decorated the same as Timmy's.

This year there was no cake. There was a celebration of sorts, sure. But what with the rumors and the rations, it wasn't possible to have such a luxury as a cake. Even candles had to be saved for more needful times. Lighting any of them, using them up, when the electricity was still working was wasteful, and the Smythe family knew it.

Slowly there had been less and less, with luxuries like sugar and beef first. They didn't miss these things anyway. They were too expensive even when times were good. But flour, and oats? That was another matter. It was a few short months before it came to that, and by then there was no denying that war was upon them. They had to conserve what they had and make do to support their boys on the front lines. They needed the food more, to fight the Nazis who were three countries away. It wasn't much to ask to have the war kept at bay. Trading a cake to have peace at home seemed like a fair trade.

But then the war came home to them.

It wasn't fair. War, and still no cake. They still were sacrificing, still saving, still rationing, and still the war came, came right to their villages, to their streets, to their doorsteps. Uncle Albert in Shropshire called their neighbor to tell them to make their way to him any way they could. They hadn't found the money for a phone since they moved to the city, and their neighbor Mr. Pete kindly passed along messages in exchange for Mama doing a little extra laundry on wash day. He'd not quite gotten the hang of it since his wife took ill with the dropsy two years back.

Mr. Smythe didn't think there was much reason to hurry. He still had a job to go to after all, and Timmy had school to see to. He was getting along so well with his classmates this term, and getting such good grades in penmanship and music. Mama Smyth didn't agree with his assessment, and said so by not saying anything. Her 'no' was simply the absence of a 'yes', as befitted a good wife to her understanding. Papa took her silence under advisement and read the newspaper more carefully, listened to the radio more closely, trying to see if there were currents under the words, perhaps telling him things were worse than the government was letting on. The slogan "Stay calm and carry on" was what tipped it. Something about it made every hair on his arms stand up. It was then that he knew they had to leave and go back home to their village of Clun as quickly as they could.

Mama was relieved, but said that going calmly was best. Best not to look like they were fleeing. That might start a panic. Just make it look like they were going on holiday.

So they packed just a few things, just enough to fit into suitcases. It wouldn't do to have too much on the train. It would call attention, and that was the last thing they wanted.

Theodore wasn't around when they left. Perhaps he had been hiding in the pantry. Perhaps he had been exploring under the bed. Even though Mama and Papa appeared calm to everyone around them, in the house they were anything but. The day they decided to leave was the day they left. No time to make up stories or have people wonder. Mama had allotted just a scant thirty minutes to pack so they couldn't over think it and try to bring too much. Timmy was so flustered he didn't realize Theodore wasn't with him until their train was outside the city gates. He fussed, sure, but Papa said they'd get him another bear. He said it in a low tone, quiet, almost but not quite gritting his teeth. Timmy had learned not to push harder when Papa spoke like this, so he gulped back his tears and distracted himself by looking at the scenery fly past his window.

It was three days later when Theodore woke to the sounds of the bomber planes. Normally, Timmy would find him at night to take him to bed with him, waking him up from his daytime slumber. Bears are awake at night. That is when they guard their young charges. But nobody in the house to wake him up meant Theodore had dozed on in a dreamless sleep, unaware of time passing.

Now he was awake, and lost. Now the city was in ruins. There were fires a few blocks over in the cathedral. The library in tatters. The school used for emergency shelter, not lessons. Now Theodore's whole being ached with the need to find Timmy. He decided to rest his head against a building for just a little while.

Can't go to sleep.

Can't go to sleep.

Must find Timmy and keep him safe.

To sleep meant to fall into that dull dreamless nothing where it is so hard to return for a Bear. To sleep might mean to lose Timmy forever.

He would rest here for just a little while, but not lie down. To lie down would be the same as death, because life without Timmy was not acceptable. A bear once turned into a Bear could not go back into that dull unfeeling world of before.

(Originally posted 11-9-15)

Edward and the turtle

Edward had always been an unusual child. His teachers expected him to become an unusual adult too. His parents? Well, that was another matter entirely.

They never said exactly how Edward came to them, or even how he came to be. Bea and Charles, Edward's parents as far as the world was aware, left town for a year a while back. When they returned, they had Edward with them. He was just over a month old they said, but some who looked in his eyes knew, just knew deep down in their bones that this child was far older in all the ways that counted. "He's an old soul" they said, not knowing how true those words were.

Of course, not everyone could see the whirling abyss of time in his eyes. It was like looking into a dark disused quarry filled with rain water. You couldn't see the bottom, and to some that was so frightening that their minds simply refused to look, to even get near. Those hidden depths spoke of secrets, of danger, of loss.

For some, Edward himself was invisible simply because of the dangerous unanswered questions that lurked like unwelcome promises behind his eyes. Their minds couldn't accept their challenge, so they simply refused to acknowledge Edward's presence, his very being. What Edward was could not be to them, so for them he was not.

Bea and Charles could see him better than anyone else, and they were grateful. They'd prayed for such a child, a "gift" as they called him, privately, fervently. The home they were living in now was a gift too, provided upon the introduction of Edward to his grandfather. For years they had scraped by, living with friends, or in trailers, or even in the library during the day and their battered

Range Rover at night. The arrival of Edward had turned their lives around for the better.

A grandchild was all Bea's father wanted from her. He promised her the house, paid off, furnished, utilities, the lot, on the day she and Charles married provided that they gave him a grandchild in due time. He made sure to explain it wasn't just any house on the table, not one of her choosing. It was to be the house by the lake on the family estate. Her sister Eloise already had the woods house, and brother Tom had been gifted the one by the cold gray boulders. Only the big house remained, and it was occupied solely by Edward's grandfather, known simply as "The Grandfather", made so by the births of all his children's children, now gathered like chicks on the family land.

Edward would have no siblings. The cost was simply too high. No money had changed hands for his conception. Money was just paper after all, just the promises of dead trees. Those who had brought Edward into the world needed something more solid than that.

Bea and Charles had been desperate to have a child, and the cost was nothing in comparison to the debt they were in. Who counts the expense when you stand to gain everything? It was like floating a check right before payday - something they knew very well.

They still didn't understand what was to be expected of them for this "gift", even though they'd signed a contract. There were fertility tests the doctors did beforehand, to make sure the couple didn't have to pay such a price, could conceive on their own, but it was to no avail. Bea suspected some of her cells were taken then, for some other cause, but she didn't dare to think about it for too long. All that mattered was that she had her child now. What happened in the future would just have to wait until then to be worried about.

Edward was always cold. Outside, on a warm July afternoon, he always wore a jacket or coat. Charles got his tailor to make a blazer for him out of the thickest tweed he could find. The colors looked like the bracken and gorse that surrounded his Uncle Tom's house. When he was inside, a fire was always going in whatever room he was in.

At first, he insisted in his own way that all the fireplaces would be working all over the house, but Bea and Charles soon realized his subtle influence over them and set some boundaries. Even as a baby he was able to make people do his will. Even without speaking he could turn them, bend them.

His parents didn't realize he was influencing their minds until the fires.

Edward had never seen a fire until he was a year old. Before that his parents bundled him up in sweaters and blankets to stop his shivering. They simply hadn't gotten around to having the chimneys inspected in that old stone house, so they had no fire out of fear. The moment they were able to light one, Edward wouldn't leave the room, delighted with his newfound unencumbered warmth. When Charles tried to remove him from the room at supper time, Edward howled and kicked Charles in the shins. Not wanting to get into a fight with his son, Charles desisted and instead brought up a tray. They all ate supper together that evening, sitting by the fire, seated on the antique Persian carpet, the arabesques and swirling flowers in the design dancing all the more by the flickering firelight. Bea thought it was charming, like a picnic.

The charm wore off after week when Edward still refused to leave the fireside. They drew him out only after they lit fires in all the other rooms. Only then would he venture from his toasty lair. After a few months though, Bea and Charles had grown tired of the constant work involved in finding seasoned wood in town and then chopping it to size. Grandfather would not allow them to cut down trees on his land, not for Edward, not for anyone. They explained to Edward that it had to be one fire from now on, in only one room, and he could wear sweaters like before if he needed to wander anywhere else in the house. He sulked for a month in that room, unwilling to get cold.

They'd not wanted all that heat, especially going from spring into summer, but Edward did, so he simply placed his thoughts over theirs, like how a voodoun priest exerts his will over a zombie. He didn't realize they would break free of his influence, his control of their actions, and certainly not so soon. For the longest time they thought they too were cold and needed the heat just like he did. It was only when Charles passed out from heat exhaustion one Tuesday that they started to question their actions, realizing that they didn't want the house to be at 92°.

From that point on they questioned everything they thought. They wondered what passed through their minds was their thought, or Edward's. He tested them to see how far his influence went. He tried simple things, like food cravings. For one week they craved bananas and they ate them like they were going out of style. A different week it was strawberries. That was a mistake, Edward soon learned, because Bea was allergic, had been since she was a child. She knew she wasn't craving them, that it had to be Edward's doing.

He had to figure out another way to get his needs met. He finally, reluctantly, decided to let them teach him their language. That dry chittering sound grated on his ears. It was so unlike the warm liquid sounds he knew as his native tongue. His mouth ached with the effort of shaping the sounds for them, but it was the only way.

When he was three they took him to get a pet. Bea decided he needed a companion. A dog was ruled out straight off the bat - the warmth Edward needed would make it lethargic at best, dead at worst. A tortoise, a Galapagos tortoise to be precise, was decided after careful and discreet inquiries with the local librarian. She explained how they are cold-blooded so they need warmth, and how they live for many years. This added quality helped to tip the scales.

The elders who had helped them hinted that their true age was far beyond their appearance. Their kind were old at birth, having already lived half a human lifetime in a middle dimension, one where they were spirit only. This gave them certain advantages. They could learn quite a bit without the bother of a body. No colds to catch, no growing pains, no accidents, no trips to the doctor or the emergency room or the morgue. They even got to skip all that awkwardness of puberty while they were learning. Only when they had gathered about 50 of our years worth of knowledge did they bother to incarnate, and only then into a bespoke body, tailored to their temperament and needs. Certainly then there were the usual risks of being embodied, but by then they knew how to navigate safely through those obstacles.

Bea and Charles only suspected at the truth behind their benefactors, the ones who had given them Edward. The Grandfather would never know. For him, Edward was of his flesh and blood and that was all he needed (or wanted) to know. No matter that Edward was decades smarter than any of his other grandchildren. If he'd known the truth about this cuckoo child, he'd throw him and his parents out and never speak their names again.

Edward was their child in deed if not in act. He never grew in Bea's womb, but he did share her DNA, as well as Charles's. The elders didn't mention there was a bit more to the mix than just the two, however.

It was kind of like fruit juice. How much actual juice was necessary for it to still be juice? Perhaps there are vitamins and minerals added to improve the quality. Perhaps other things to make it last longer. Sure, at the end it still looked and tasted like juice, but really only 50% of it was straight from the vine. It was kind of like that with Edward and his parents, but in their case it was more like 5% than 50%. They'd never be the wiser. Edward was theirs, and that was all they cared about. And of course, they were parents in the way that mattered most - they loved him, took care of him, and make sure he was happy and wanted for nothing.

Well, they didn't give him everything. That would spoil him. And after all, they still had to make sure he wasn't using the old mind push on them.

(Originally posted 11-11-15)

Taxidermy for amateurs

Emma had no way of knowing how her experiment in home taxidermy would work out until she tried. She'd read up about it in a correspondence course, changing her name to Eugene on the paperwork. No self-respecting school would teach a woman how to do such work, especially if they knew how she planned to use this knowledge.

She'd started simple - a dead raccoon she found near the edge of the field. A bird who'd gotten too close to a stray cat. It was unfortunate that the possum she'd spotted just down the road from the farm was too far gone, the turkey vultures having gotten first dibs. Sure, she still could have practiced on the mangy thing, but she wanted her artwork to look natural, or as natural as the deceased can look.

It took her two and a half years to work up the courage to try on a human. This had been her plan all along, but she had to be sure of her skill before she tried something so bold. Even men wouldn't be so presumptuous as to step into that field of work without official license.

Emma knew too many folks in the village who went into debt over having to bury their dead. There was no good reason to spend a year's income on someone who couldn't appreciate it. New fancy clothes for someone who could never afford better than hand-me-downs his whole life? Nonsense. Silk lined coffin to sleep in, when cotton sheets were just fine all their life? Ludicrous.

And worst of all was all those chemicals pumped into their veins to keep them fresh for whenever Jesus got around to making a return visit. When he came, he'd better have a shovel, a jackhammer, and a pair of wire cutters to help them out after he woke them from their slumber. 6 feet down stuck in a concrete vault and a locked coffin was bad enough. Their mouth wired shut (to avoid any unpleasantness during the viewing) would make life difficult for the newly reanimated. Who wanted to come back from the dead like that?

Emma had another plan, a kinder, cheaper plan. Taxidermy. Dry out Grandpa Ross or Uncle Seymour so he doesn't develop a case of the rot, and prop him up in a chair in the living room. Much cheaper, and he'd still be around to chat with. When the second coming happened he'd be just as ready as anyone else.

(Originally posted 2-4-16)

The erasure

They finally came. After months of broadcasts on all known media (radio, television, Internet, newspaper, shortwave, telegraph, TTY, dolphins, psychics) saying it was coming, that they were coming, it had finally happened.

Nobody knew who was sending the broadcasts, or where they were from. Agencies and detectives and amateur sleuths all over the world tried to answer those questions, to no avail. Séances were held. Runes were consulted. Wires were tapped. Still the messages came, and still no one knew the source or the author. Television anchors were told to say nothing that might frighten the public more than they already were. Talk show hosts were, as usual, under no authority or ethical standard, so they said whatever they felt, regardless of truth or concern for how their prattlings would harm.

The beings, or spirits, or aliens, or whatever they were had tried to communicate with our earth for far longer than people realized. They had subtly influenced moods and desires since before 2000, like a silent alarm, like an odorless poison. They were the reason for the Y2K panic. They were the reason preppers stocked up on ammunition and canned ham. They were the reason people began to mis-trust the authorities and began to take matters into their own hands. Urban farms, homeschooling, anti-vaccine? These were their doing. Layer by layer they had painted a picture of paranoia in our brains to divide us, keep us off balance.

Everyone was affected to some degree. It was only those who didn't consume mass media that maintained some semblance of control over their actions. All those who watched TV or movies or listened to the radio got multiple doses of the message, and it was cumulative, just like any other poison. A single bee sting is annoying, but not fatal. A thousand stings is another matter.

When they finally came it was almost a relief.

It was a cool day in August, one of those days that was not too hot or humid with a few clouds in the azure sky. The morning had gone peacefully for everyone for a change. The disturbing dreams have finally stopped. Even the news reports were calm for a change, with the latest plastic surgery of one celebrity being the lead instead of the usual threats of war from petty tyrants trying to get the world to notice them. It was shaping up to be a beautiful day, until the skies scissored open with the dimension melting sight/sound/smell of their ships at 11:11 AM.

People started to see sounds and hear colors.

Time ran backwards and sideways and then stopped.

Everything suddenly made sense

but there were no words

anymore to explain it.

And then there was nothing.

The silence was thicker than the darkest night, a crushing subterranean weight, more alienating than being trapped in the Marianas Trench in a powerless submarine.

Then, just as suddenly, there was only now. The past wasn't even a memory. It was just a word. All mistakes, all forgotten grocery lists, all insults, all arguments, gone in a blink of the eye. Gone too were first kisses. baby's first laugh, that perfect day in October when the sky is the blue of watery dreams and crisp like a Gala apple.

All of it.

Gone.

Somehow they knew, whoever they were. They knew that what was holding us back was our near-pathological need to catalog the past into neat (and not so neat) piles, holding onto memories and snapshots and train tickets and receipts for ice skates and ice cream. Somehow they knew that our need to separate those piles into "good" and "bad" was our secret un-doing, our un-humaning, our un-being. Somehow they knew that our "bad" pile held us down, became a pattern for our future, made us think we would always be cheated, be robbed, be abandoned. Somehow too, they knew that our "good" pile equally enslaved us, making us feel that we could never feel that exhilarated or proud or delighted ever again.

Our collective and individual past being erased was as great a blessing to us as a tornado or a house fire. It forced us to stop holding onto the dried husks of what it means to be truly alive. For too long we thought that the artificial joy of our memories was what made us human.

Overnight, the scrapbooking industry was rendered irrelevant. No one could even imagine why they had spent so much of their lives (and money) gluing memorabilia into organized books, accented with metallic rickrack and die-cut stickers. No one took photographs either, choosing to see their lives through their own eyes rather than through a viewfinder.

Why save the past anymore?

It was meaningless.

Only the present moment,

a moment eternally composed

of beginnings,

was valid.

In that moment

anything

could happen.

(Originally posted 2-5-16)

Felix's last stand

Felix was having none of it. His parents had chased him around the house for an hour, trying to snatch him up. This was the day to get his hair cut for the first time.

They had braced him for it for a week - dropping hints as to what to expect, offering promises of treats if he behaved. He knew full well what they were planning to do to him. He knew that of all the things they had done to him in the name of his 'best interest', this was the last straw. He had to finally draw the line.

He was sick of being directed, ordered, bossed around. Nobody ever asked him what he wanted to wear. Nobody even cared to know what he wanted to eat. Every day of his three years of being alive was a battle of wills.

Every now and then they got it right and they gave him something that wasn't tasteless to eat or scratchy to wear. Those days were rare, and on every other dull, grueling day, he felt that his very being was being washed away bit by bit until the rock that he was had worn away to nothingness.

Little Maxie was his only friend, the only one who understood. They'd gotten her when Felix was six months old after a particularly difficult trip to the doctor for booster shots. They hoped she would be a calming influence on him. It turned out that the two had developed a stronger bond than his parents could ever imagine. They both felt the same way.

Both were ordered around. Both were ignored, neglected, relegated to the 'passive' pile in their parent's minds. Felix and Maxie developed a common bond out of their silent mutual suffering.

They forged a method of communication that worked perfectly for them, which his parents were oblivious to. Why wouldn't they be? They never even thought to speak with either one of them - always at, or to, but never with.

It was funny in a not-so-funny kind of way. Both of his parents were all about communication, but they never thought to apply their skills at home. Mom spent her weekdays teaching dolphins how to communicate, getting them to mimic human speech or to point at symbol boards with their noses or flippers. All day she taught them how to tell her what they were feeling. She constantly modified her techniques to better understand their needs and wishes and thoughts. Never once did she think to learn their language.

These 'animals', these beings she and every other scientist thought were lesser than, purely by virtue of the fact they weren't human, were expected to learn human language rather than the other way around. Who was less intelligent?

Felix's Dad was equally culpable. He too had no excuse. They both knew better and they both didn't act upon their knowledge. Ignorance was indeed bliss, but they didn't have that luxury.

His Dad worked as a counselor with people who had learning disabilities. It had been his passion for a dozen years, far longer than his marriage, a third of his life. He'd even gotten professional recognition for his techniques to reach patients who were considered unreachable by conventional methods.

Neither of the parents thought to take their work home with them. Felix was a child, and that was that. It was unthinkable to them that he should be asked his opinion. Dolphins and profoundly autistic children were paid more heed than him, purely because he was theirs. The idea of trying to communicate with their child was something they never would have considered. Why would they ask him his opinion? They knew that their job as parents was to tell him what to think – not to ask.

Felix and Maxie had refused to budge from the settee. That stiff sofa was the ultimate symbol of all they were fighting against. It had been moved into Felix's room last winter when the parents had bought a plush leather sofa for themselves. They had decided unequivocally that dogs and children were not allowed on it, out of fear of stains and rips. They were relegated to the board-stiff contraption of cloth and wood that had been in the family longer than anybody could remember. It had stains but no stuffing. In their minds it was perfect for a boy and his dog - they couldn't wreck it any more than it was.

The boy and his dog thought otherwise. Here they were going to make their final stand. Here was going to be the epicenter of their future, the point where they were going to make their captors listen to them for the first time.

In unison they both peed on the couch.

Horrified, Felix's parents and Maxie's owner (or was it the other way around?) stared at them both as the warm pungent liquid seeped into the threadbare cloth. As a communication technique, it wasn't the best. It got them to be noticed for sure, but not taken as seriously as they had hoped.

(Originally posted 2-11-16)

Twins

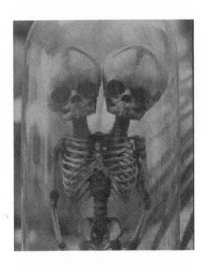

Their mother had always wanted twins, but not like this. Carol's biological clock was winding down about the time her life was picking up. When she finally had the time, money, and energy to have children, she'd gotten too old to even consider having multiple pregnancies. She wanted at least two children for the same reason people brought home two puppies or kittens - they would always have a playmate. With time slipping away on her, having twins seemed like the best option.

She never even considered adoption. The children had to be hers. She knew that down to her bones. The idea of "family legacy" was so firmly imprinted onto her identity that taking in somebody else's unwanted children was out of the question. It wasn't even on the table. It wasn't even in the room.

She couldn't afford to chance it. So she went to the local medicine/miracle worker. The gnarled old being was a fixture of the community that everybody knew about but nobody talked about. She? He? Who knew? At that age it was impossible to tell. His? Her? voice was raspy and the clothes were baggy enough to conceal whatever shape s/he might have. Nobody knew, and everyone was afraid to ask. "Doctor" was the being's title as well as name. Fortunately this language didn't differentiate gender in its words or it would have been more awkward. Undefined gender seemed somehow appropriate for this profession, one of yes/and, of greys, of liminal spaces, of betweens. The Doctor's unusual shop/office/home was like that as well, beyond definition.

Carol had written a letter asking for an appointment. This was how it was done, how it always had been done. The Doctor felt that websites were too fiddly, too impersonal. The message would get lost. Even phone lines were eschewed.

Ideally, the client (never "patient") would happen to meet the Doctor while they were both out doing errands in the village markets. A lot could be done to further the desired outcome if both of them were on the same time-line. Never quite syncing up was a bad sign. But, communicating by letters was a good second choice.

They agreed upon Wednesday the third, at 11:30 in the morning. The Doctor arranged visits by feel, rather than by any usual method. It was the same as how a safecracker worked, or a dowser, or a chef. It was all by feel. No astrology charts or Ouija boards or runes. No Day Planners either. There was never a receptionist or assistant. The Doctor's motto was do it all yourself, or don't do it at all. Too many cooks spoil the broth, and all that.

Carol left her house that Wednesday morning very excited and hopeful. She wore her favorite red jumper and galoshes even though the weather forecast promised a partly sunny day with only a 10% chance of snow flurries. They were her favorite galoshes, purchased used at the corner Oxfam three years back. She'd always had great luck when she wore them, so they seemed to fit the bill for the day. She even asked off from work for the rest of the afternoon so she could get started right away on whatever course of action the Doctor recommended.

Everything the Doctor did was by suggestion or recommendation - never an order, never even a request. Everything had to be voluntary. The client had to be a part of the process, never acted upon, but with. If the Doctor decided it was possible to effect a change there was always a list of recommendations. It wasn't always possible to obtain or do all of them, either due to the time of year or available resources. The client, if accepted, (not a given) would then go out armed with that list.

Instructions could include such varied examples as "Stand barefoot on a newly harvested field for 10 minutes, facing west. Be sure not to be noticed. This must be done sometime between the hours of 8 AM and 3 PM." Or perhaps something like: "Buy and eat some kind of fruit you have never eaten before." Or maybe even: "Write down your greatest hope for your future on a piece of borrowed paper. Set it afloat on a stream." Generally, at least two of the three options must be done, in whatever way the client could. The "how" was up to interpretation, and was part of the cure.

Wearing a certain color for a week (at least) was a common request, although the color changed with the task at hand. Often this was how other people in the community knew you were under the Doctor's care. They never would ask, though, out of respect, or perhaps fear. It was difficult to not be noticed when someone started wearing shades of teal or salmon or magenta, especially day after day.

Almost immediately after having sex that Friday night a month later, Carol knew she was pregnant. She didn't dare breathe a word of it to her partner for fear she might jinx it. She didn't even go to the pharmacy to get a pregnancy test for the same reason.

She wasn't sure where her self-imposed superstition came from, and that might have caused the aberration. Maybe it was the galoshes. Maybe the orientation of her bed. Maybe she didn't follow the list correctly.

Later, after the birth, the Doctor consulted with Carol. They both looked at the babies (baby?). They went over everything she did, everything she ate, everything she thought. She was sure she had the right intention during the act. It had been all she'd been thinking about for months, so how could it be anything else? Two babies in one pregnancy.

The Doctor had been very insistent with her that intention was important for all pregnancies, but especially for hers since it was so specific. The Doctor explained that ideally, people would have sex only when they wanted to have a child, and then they would do it mindfully and prayerfully. The moment of conception was when the soul chose to incarnate. This is a delicate and perilous time. There were many souls about, of all kinds, waiting to enter a body. Some entered at conception. That was ideal.

Others chose to take up residence afterwards. This resulted in what psychiatrists called "multiple personality disorder". Priests called it "possession". New Agers called it "walk-ins". It was all the same thing, and it was all less than desirable.

The Doctor explained that ideally the potential parents would pray before having sex, alerting the souls, the beings-in-waiting, that an opening, a doorway if you will, was being created for them. The parents would meditate on the characteristics and personality of the child that they hoped to welcome into their lives. They would speak about what kind of home they could provide.

In a way it was like a blind date, or perhaps more like an arranged marriage. They were going to be together a long time. It was important to do this well, rather than leave it to chance.

The trouble is, too many people didn't think it all before having sex. It was as if they were swept away, like they were in a stagecoach, and the horses got spooked. Before they realized what was happening, they were where they hadn't planned on being, because they hadn't planned. Sometimes they got stuck there. Just like with marriage, it is a good idea to choose wisely before this long-term commitment.

Too many babies were being born without souls properly attached to them because of this. Some had very weak souls and had sensory or neurological disorders because they weren't fully in the body. Some souls weren't even human.

But that wasn't the problem here. Carol and her partner had prayed for two souls, alright. The only problem is that they somehow ended up with two souls in one body. This wasn't uncommon, but could take different forms. The obstetrician had explained that sometimes twins are conceived but one is absorbed. The result? One baby, but it might have its twin as a vestigial part of its body, in the abdominal area, for instance.

Or if the fusing is complete, it will have chimerism. Or in this case, conjoined. The obstetrician couldn't explain why this had happened, but the Doctor could, after consulting with the souls of the twins.

Twins were wanted, and twins came. They were twins in the truest sense this incarnation. They were two, but one. When they were in spirit form, they were separate but they wanted to always be together.

In their previous incarnation they had been twins in the usual sense. That family had also wanted twins, but shortly after their birth the father had gotten laid off from his job. The economy had taken a downturn and he had difficulty finding another job. Months went by and the savings grew smaller. Their mother grew more and more exhausted with caring for them and with worry.

Finally the decision was made. It was the same decision that some families made about their pets under similar circumstances. They were "given away to good homes". Unfortunately in this case, they were separate ones. The children always felt that half of their very being was missing from that point onwards.

After their deaths, they had waited a long time to find another family that wanted twins. This time, they wanted to make sure they couldn't be separated ever again.

(Originally posted 2-15-16)

Tracy and Robin

Tracy and Robin had joked for years before they got married that people never knew who was "he" and who was "she" of the two of them. They decided that it was nobody's business, so they never let on.

Their friends had hoped to learn the truth on their wedding day. Surely they would wear the traditional clothes? They were in for quite a surprise when they arrived at the event. They wore the traditional clothes, but not in the traditional way. This was in line with everything they stood for, so it made sense after all, but it still didn't answer any questions.

Tracy and Robin were drawn to each other not out of a sense of finding their other half, but in finding another person who was whole. Both were perfectly comfortable repairing a car or knitting a shawl. Both could mow the lawn as well as cook. They felt lucky that their parents had taught them both how to be people first and foremost. Their gender was never used as a reason for or against learning anything.

They both hid their gender, not out of a sense of privacy or shame, but out of a sense of rightness. They wanted people to relate to them as people. The first item of prejudice was gender. Sure, you could add race, religion, creed, national origin and a host of other things up to and including what football team they rooted for. People used any excuse they could to pigeonhole you, to decide who you were before you even opened your mouth. Tracy and Robin figured that the more you can avoid those markers, the more people would have to make up their own minds for a change.

They were mindful to shop only where the bathrooms were genderless. Sometimes the buildings were old and only had one restroom with a single toilet. Sometimes they had family restrooms. They didn't want to have to out themselves if they could avoid it.

They shopped at thrift stores, getting whatever clothing that struck their fancy and wasn't too snug. Both were equally comfortable in pants or skirts. They were pleased when they could find clothing that was from immigrants because it was often loose and ambiguous. Comfort was the most important thing.

It was always assumed that one was female, but it wasn't a given. Both could have been. Or neither. Or one or both could be intersex. Did it matter? Nobody separates by eye color or height, so why separate by something as equally meaningless and random as gender?

(Originally posted 2-20-16)

Mr Michaels

Mr Michaels' blindness was absolute. Born sighted, it had been 20 years before the cataracts had begun to form from the kiss of sunlight.

It happened so slowly at first, like a fog creeping in on cat's paws. Every month the dull haze thickened, coalesced just a little more. It was so gradual that he never even realized his sight was being stolen from him until it was gone. It was as if his sight was a stone and the sun was the sea, washing it away to nothingness, no trace of it ever having been there.

It was nothing to Mr Michaels. His sight had gone so gradually that he'd forgotten he'd ever had vision. Just like that sea-stone, all evidence of its existence was erased. Just as slowly and just as insistently, his memory of sight had dissolved as well. He could no longer remember his mother's face or the color of the sky in early November, could no longer even remember that he had ever known these things.

He didn't think of his blindness as an absence. He didn't think of it at all.

All his life he had worked outside. Perhaps it was an undiagnosed case of claustrophobia. Perhaps he was just set in his ways. His first job had been in landscaping, and every one after that had been related. Grounds crew for a municipal park, another one helping harvest apples, it was all the same to him, as long as he was outside.

His father never knew if he'd ever tried for anything more advanced. He never asked, but he'd been tempted to often. He wanted to encourage him to be his best rather than settle, but he remembered his own father doing the same to him and he still resented him for it. Perhaps this was his best? Perhaps he led a simple life because he was simple? Best not to dig too deeply.

Mr Michael's hands became his eyes, showing him the size of the bulb or seed that he held. He then knew how far down to dig to plant it. His hands told him where the weeds were to pluck, told him what apples were ready to harvest and which ones were best left for the birds. His feet told him how far the flower bed was from the orchard, how far from the stables. His nose told him whether the horses were sick or scared. His ears told him whether a storm was coming, and whether it was going to be strong enough to warrant bringing the animals in early.

Watching him work, you'd never know he was blind. By tacit agreement, all the other workers on the farm kept everything where it had always been. That one incident with the misplaced hay bale had been enough to convince them.

It was only when you looked directly into his eyes that you knew beyond a shadow of a doubt that he was blind. Very few people were brave enough to do this more than once. Looking into his milky eyes was like looking into a pair of mirrors set just opposite each other. All you could see was yourself, all of yourself, unto eternity, ever diminishing into meaninglessness. It was overwhelming and humbling. You could see all of your strengths and all of your faults, unvarnished, untampered by the usual lies you told yourself. This alone was unsettling, but the additional feature of his gaze was to leave you with an overwhelming sense of your utter insignificance.

Mr Michaels was completely unaware of this. He wasn't bothered in the slightest that people tended to leave him alone. It meant he had time for his own amusements. That suited him just fine.

(Originally posted 2-20-16)

Rosie's Adjustable Man

Rosie knew what she wanted in a man. Trouble was, she wanted something different every day. The wealthier ladies could afford different models, but they had room to store them too. She'd had to settle for a model with adjustable heads. The body stayed the same, but the personality changed. It wasn't ideal, but it worked. Currently she had six different versions, but over thirty were available. Whenever she could afford it, she got a new head for her Adjustable Man.

Rosie's house wasn't tiny by any means. It was the standard allotment for Zeta-class citizens - three bedrooms and one large common area with dining/ kitchen/ living room, with movable panels to divide up the areas when necessary. This was a far cry from Gamma-class, with only two bedrooms and a living room but no kitchen. That was shared, communal style, with ten other Gammas.

Gammas tended to eat together in the common dining room. Slinking off to eat in their private apartments, hunched over a coffee table while sitting on a stiff sofa, was possible but frowned upon. Nobody would say anything about it to the citizen who did it, but then they simply wouldn't say anything at all to them for a few days afterwards.

It wasn't planned that way. It wasn't a rule. It was more like a habit, or tradition. Not sharing time with your fellow citizens meant you wanted to be alone, so they gave each other space at those times. But, if a citizen was absent more than about four times a month and wasn't on a scheduled trip for their task-group, then subtle and not-so-subtle inquiries were made. Some were to the citizen's family. Some were to the Overseers. Perhaps s/he was ill? Perhaps therapy needed to be assigned? Perhaps s/he needed to be reclassified? Sometimes that particular area's citizen class wasn't a good fit for that citizen's style of life. Never would they ask a Gamma-class citizen themselves if anything was wrong. That wasn't thinkable, not for that class. It was only once you were promoted to Zeta-class that you were even considered to have enough spirit to have an opinion.

Rosie had opinions all the time, and felt that everyone needed to hear them. The Overseer channeled this into encouraging her to write an online blog, where she felt that she was being heard for a change. She thought she was making a difference. She was wrong. Nobody read her writing. The numbers on the statistics were a ruse from the Overseer to get her to keep writing and thus keep her out of the way. The comments were supplied by workers in his office. It kept her placated and maintained order. It didn't do to have citizens thinking too much. It upset the social fabric.

She was so opinionated that no man wanted to spend time with her, and so insecure that she didn't want to spend time with herself. Fortunately for her, she was not alone in this. Plenty of women had been told "You think too much" by men, and rather than stop thinking, or at least out loud, they decided to get an Adjustable Man. He could be modified in any way imaginable, providing you had the resources.

It was easy these days to pick up a used version, have the memory wiped, and start from scratch. Or, you could custom build one online and have it shipped to you, ready to cook, mow the yard, and be pleasant to take on a visit with your friends. No more awkward times like when your man suddenly started talking about less-than-polite topics around your best friends or coworkers. No more attitude about doing housework or it being "woman's work". No, the days of men thinking their contribution to the family ended as soon as they left their workplace ended around the time women realized they didn't have to have children, and thus didn't have to stay home to raise them.

Adjustable Women were in the works for those women who wanted to work outside of the home after having children. There were never enough reliable or affordable childcare providers - never had been. Come to think of it, the same was true for eldercare. Nobody wanted to take care of the very young or the very old for very long, even if they weren't related to them. Those that did wanted a lot of money for it, or they had less than honorable reasons for seeking those jobs. But Adjustable Women were proving to be harder to make than Adjustable Men.

Rosie was trying to decide who she wanted as her partner to the dance tonight. It was almost as important as determining what dress to wear. Too formal? Too casual? She wished there was a guideline on the RSVP, like "black tie" or "blue jeans" but for partners. She'd hate to take a stuffy, know-it-all partner to a casual gathering, the same as she'd hate to take a sci-fi geek, able to name all Star Trek captains in order (and delineate their flaws and charms) to a company luncheon. How did early-century escorts do it?

She opted for the boring "Bob" version. He was cute, but he didn't talk much. Her friends would understand, and the new people she was there to meet wouldn't care.

(Originally posted 2-23-16)

Pod people

Nell was having none of it. Not anymore. Her husband simply refused to even try to breathe air. The doctor said he could, that his lungs could adapt to this environment, but he disagreed. Trouble was, he'd never know unless he tried.

Elowyn had read about other Marenians who had converted to air breathing. He'd never met one, of course. How could he? There were only three who lived in this state, and the closest was two hours away by plane. No airline would let him on a plane with his argon suit, that was a given. Their fears were unproven, but policy was policy.

They'd met three years ago at the landing site. She was a reporter, alerted by the scanner in the office that something was coming from the skies again. That scanner was worth its cost from all the leads it provided. Quick as a wink she was downstairs and in her car, trying to not drive off the road as she followed the plumes of green clouds stretching like a tightrope from the eastern sky to some nearby cornfield - Mr. O'Reilly's, most likely. He had the biggest one, so it stood to reason. She turned down Ellis Way and got there before the locals did. Farmers listened to the scanner same as reporters did, and for much the same reason. It was the best way to know what was going on that might be of interest. Something like this would pull them out of their barns for sure.

Just think of it! Aliens! Here! In Mill City!

Nell had guessed the pod's trajectory right and reached the small crater it created just after the police had gotten there. The ground was still steaming next to the blue (metal?) craft. She noticed that there was a bright iridescent sheen across the pod's surface, reflecting the late afternoon summer sun, as well as a distinctive sharp smell much like ammonia, but she couldn't quite place it.

They didn't know at the time but it turned out that the color and the smell were both hallmarks of the Marenians. They both came about because their ships were alive, growing out of the same stuff as the people. This way they could self-repair. It saved a lot of money and time that way. It worked perfectly as long as they stayed in the Marenian solar system because the elements were more or less the same throughout.

Earth, however, was another matter entirely. The stresses of the previous crashes had resulted in every pod going into automatic repair mode, sending wispy tendrils into the soil to gather the raw materials needed to boil up replacement parts in the integral kitchen/lab. Three minutes after the tendrils went down, they came back up, spit out what dirt they'd sampled, and retracted back into the beetle-like shell, refusing to budge. The self-preservation instinct was the strongest one, so the pods calmly explained in their proto-language to the pilot inside them that the soil was not compatible with their electrochemical makeup, so repairs would not be forthcoming. As trained, each pod then sent out a trans-space summons for another pod to make the trek to bring dirt from home so repairs could proceed.

The only problem was that these supply pods came and they too became stranded. They'd underestimated the amount of dirt needed for the repairs. The pods were small, with barely enough room for the pilot. Even if they were able to navigate without a pilot there still wouldn't have been enough room for dirt to repair both ships.

No matter – flying without a pilot wasn't an option. Each pod was raised with its pilot from the moment s/he was formerly admitted to the astro-nav program. Saying that they were synchronized wasn't the half of it. Cells were harvested from under the tongue of the pilot and cultured over three weeks, growing into a ship that learned as the pilot learned. This was no simple cloning. The two beings were separate in body only. All past, present, and future were shared.

This created a dilemma when the pods, and thus the pilots, began to be stranded. Without hope of repair, the pods chose to self-terminate, opting for a quick death over a slow lingering one. The pilots had to be tranquilized before the pods could self-euthanize. Otherwise it would have been too painful for them to endure. Some later, once they'd learned the local language, said it was like amputation of half your limbs and your brain. Many were encouraged to adopt dogs afterwards as the closest Earth option to the deep connection that they had shared with the ships.

Nell had worked closely with Elowyn after the crash, helping him to adjust to Earth living. There was no going back to Marenia, so he had to learn a whole different culture. This was made easier because of his astro-nav training, but it was still understandably difficult.

She'd not planned on adopting a stray, but the Mayor assured her that she was the most qualified person in the city for the job. Simply being a reporter, curious about new things, made her ideal, he said. Put that way, how could she refuse? It was a high honor to be deemed worthy of helping a stranded Marenian. You were serving as an ambassador for the whole planet, after all. The future of the relationship between the two solar systems would be created from these one-on-one relationships.

It was about a year later that they both realized that they were quite compatible together and decided to formalize their pairing. Fortunately for them, other human-Marenian pairs had formed before they had even met, and laws had been changed to allow for interspecies marriage. There was only one difference with these marriages and all others – one member of the union had to be sterilized. Doctors weren't comfortable with what could happen if a child was created.

There was no way a child could have been created in the case of Nell and Elowyn. He was still hermetically sealed inside his argon suit. He had to have it to breathe on Earth, he insisted. The material in the suit was fortunately impervious to decay, or he would have a more difficult time of it.

Nell was quietly upset when she learned this, hoping that he'd eventually be forced to adapt to Earth ways. She loved him, of course, but she thought that things would be better for both of them if he didn't wear that darned suit. It made going out to visit friends awkward. Plus, the smell took some getting used to. The ammonia-like smell was a byproduct of the impervious material. It was unnoticeable on Marenia, but on Earth it alerted others that there was a foreigner around even before they saw him. It made some people not want to deal with Marenians at all, saying that they smelled like used gym socks.

Nell and Elowyn mostly kept to themselves at home when she wasn't working. He didn't have to work – none of the stranded pilots did. They didn't need food, and they weren't interested in owning anything. If they couldn't carry it, they didn't need it – this philosophy was part and parcel of being a Marenian. It was how they had finally adapted to a planet with too many people and not enough land. They didn't even need to live in homes anymore, having selectively bred themselves over twenty-three generations to be unaffected by temperature changes or ultraviolet rays. Some did live in homes on Marenia out of habit or convenience, and most pilots on Earth did as well, but it wasn't uncommon to see one hanging out with homeless people under overpasses or near street corners. They were comfortable wherever they happened to be.

The Marenians got along with the homeless population uncommonly well. They had in common their philosophy of "less is more", albeit perhaps unwillingly for some of the homeless. Soon the Marenians and homeless had developed a spiritual system - not a religion - about this, encouraging others to get rid of their addiction to things. They explained that there was a reason that the Earth language used the word "possession" to refer to things as well as being taken over by demons.

It had to be a spiritual system because a religion would require stuff – books or buildings, for instance, and this was totally opposed to their beliefs. Of course, many years later, after the founders had died and no more new Marenians came to Earth, their simple way was converted like all other spiritual paths had been and there were not only cathedrals to "less is more" but also gift shops with plastic trinkets made in China.

(Originally posted 3-14-16)

Melissa's story

Melissa knew it was time to leave her job when her boss sent her that email. Nearly 20 years with the same firm and it all came down to one thing - trust. She simply didn't trust him to be honest. Or fair. Or rational. He was her third boss, but they were all the same. All toed the party line, all had degrees in "CYA". Normally, she would have put her head down, not drawn any attention, and soon things would blow over or the manager would retire or get transferred.

It took her six years to realize that her job, while saying that it cared for its employees, didn't back that up with real action. The bullies and incompetents got the management positions. They wrote the performance reviews too, and they were all one-way. All the reviews were top-down, so the subordinates never had a say in how they were being managed. This was the norm all over, so it never occurred to her that it was wrong, never occurred to her that it was possible to change it.

Her friend Bobby had died because of it. He'd drunk himself to death over anxiety and fear, too much stress and a job he had to have to pay his mortgage and his alimony. He managed to work up the momentum to leave the sinking ship of his marriage, but his job was another matter. He was dead three days before he was found. In many ways it was three years.

Melissa wasn't going to go out like that. She wasn't going to give her boss the pleasure of knowing he'd won with his squirrely ways. She ran over Paul Simon's song in her head for options. Hop on the bus? Make a new plan? Drop off the keys? Well, she wasn't leaving a lover, but it still sounded like a good exit strategy. And, after all, she had been screwed.

The email that morning said it all without saying anything. She'd asked for some time off. Her only joy now was looking forward to vacations, yet she was told, in writing, that her request did not meet his guidelines. There was also a mention that this was her second attempt to violate this policy. The only problem was that it wasn't written policy. It certainly wasn't corporate policy. And he did not say at the time that it was his policy, but just a guideline. She had no way of knowing that she'd stepped over some line into dangerous territory.

He told her more with that email than simply "no". By putting it in writing, his not-so-veiled threat was made clear. Two violations, without the first one even being intentional, meant that three and you're out. What nonsense. How could she have known she broke a rule the first time she did it when he hadn't told her the guidelines? Heck, he hadn't even given her a list of her job duties. Suddenly she was one step away from trouble. It was like driving on a road that had dangerous curves and no guard rails and no warning signs.

He was a squirrel. That was certain. Everybody knew that he was a manager in title only. The problem was that nobody bothered to tell him. So he sent passive aggressive emails rather than confronting people directly. He didn't manage. There was no plan or direction. He didn't lead. Well, he led by negatives. Don't do what he does. He didn't even know what people did for their jobs, so how could he manage them?

Melissa took a breath in and reminded herself that Jesus said only God is above us. Don't follow people. If you do, you are saying that they are more important than God is. To follow a person, no matter who they are - brother, father, aunt, boss, teacher, minister, spouse, governor, president, - anybody - was to make them into an idol.

She often wondered why she had so many bad bosses, so many who let the power go to their heads and quit working. It wasn't fair that they got paid four times what so she did yet did a fourth of the work. It's like they forgot what it was like to be a subordinate.

Perhaps that was the problem. Where could she work with there were no was no hierarchy? She left the social group she was in because of that kind of bullying. She left the church too for the very same reason, among many others. Over and over again she kept hitting that wall. The lesson wasn't learned yet, apparently.

She'd waited out bad bosses before. How long until he retired? But deep down, she knew that if she didn't learn the lesson with this one, it would resurface with another one.

Back to Jesus. What does he say? First, give thanks for the situation because it reminded her to pray and seek his help. Sometimes that was as far she got in her prayer, but now she knew there was more.

Jesus said that before you take your offerings to the Temple that if you have issue with anyone, you must leave your offering and go make things right. But how was she to do that? She was starting out in the negative. And she wasn't even the one who had caused the problem. Her boss was in the wrong. This was backwards.

She remembered that story in the Bible when David was small and had no armor. With God's power he killed Goliath with just one stone. Not even a sword. Anything was possible with God on your side.

Would talking with him make him feel threatened and thus worsen her standing? She knew she'd get no backup from higher up in the corporation. She's gone that route before with an even worse manager. She still had unresolved trauma from that time.

There'd be no help from her husband, either. He was even more bullied in his past. He couldn't be objective.

So she was alone, again. Sure she had Jesus, and God, and the Holy Spirit. That had to count for something, right? But they weren't physically here. They couldn't go talk to him for her, or find her another job, or kill him off, or magically change everything. Perhaps that was the point too.

Perhaps Jesus came and said all that he did to tell her to not even have him above her, but within her, to give her the strength to do it herself. She wasn't alone, then. She was doubled. Enhanced. There was a synergy, more than the sum of the parts.

But she still didn't know what to do. Wait, and seem passive? Or wait until there is a clear path, a plan, and instruction from God? In the past, she always found herself doing the right thing, like a puppet, motivated by God. This current problem was a jigsaw puzzle and she didn't have all the pieces yet, but God always does.

Was this event shifting her away from this job? Was it right to stay in a place, work 40 hours, and not feel like she fit? Had she outgrown it? It isn't like she married this job.

It wasn't "till death do you part". It certainly wasn't for richer.

She prayed some more, and then she knew what to do. She was grateful that even though God doesn't provide a map for life, God most certainly provided a compass. With her heart focused on God, she knew she could walk through any situation, knowing that it would come out the way it was supposed to be.

(Originally posted 3-23-16)

Little Jake and the chicken

Little Jake Royce hated his chicken. He wanted a dog, the same as Billy had. His Ma said "If Billy jumped off a bridge, would you do that too?" Little Jake was only four but he already knew not to answer that question. There were some questions that had no answers. There were some, however, that if you didn't answer you got a spanking.

But not at Little Jake's house. They never spanked him, never would. Ma and Pa would talk to him if he broke some house rule. They'd use reason and explain how he was violating the social contract. They'd express how sad they were about his poor choices. This was of course when they actually noticed what he was doing. Most of the time they let him do whatever he wanted.

His parents had both been raised by missionaries. While they liked the wildness of not having a fixed address, they couldn't stand the rules. Do this. Don't do that. Whether it was about God or chores made no difference. They both craved unending vistas of freedom as children, so when they finally had a child of their own, they gave it to him. Except when it came to that chicken.

In general, he could do whatever he pleased. He could stay up as late as he wanted, learn or not learn his numbers and letters whenever the mood struck him, or eat hot dogs and popcorn for three weeks in a row. They wanted him to be free to live his life. He still wasn't potty trained and they were delighted, saying it was oppressive to insist a child do anything he wasn't ready for. Of course, how could he be ready? He didn't even know it was an option. He thought it was normal to poop wherever and whenever you wanted. He thought that his parents didn't need to go as often as he did because they were so big. They had more room to store it.

He never understood what they were doing when they said they were going to "step down the hall". The bathroom was where you had a bath, and that was it. Not like he had one of those very often, either.

But the chicken was not a debatable issue. If he had to have a pet, it had to be a chicken. Both his parents were allergic to anything with fur, so dogs and cats were out. Even hamsters weren't okay. Ferrets weren't even considered. Even if they didn't have fur, the smell was a real turn-off.

Hattie the hen and Reggie the rooster lived next-door at the co-op. Little Jake liked Hattie better (when forced to choose between a rock and a hard place), but his parents thought it was like supporting an indentured servant to have a hen - all that egg-laying. She wasn't free like a rooster to their minds. So that Monday, Reggie the rooster came home, seemingly pleased as punch to have a whole yard to himself. It didn't take long for him to make a roost for himself in Little Jake's favorite climbing tree. His parents took it as a sign that they were going to get along famously. Little Jake took it as a sign that the rooster liked pooping on his head. This made Little Jake think that maybe it was time to learn how to use the potty. He couldn't be upstaged by a rooster.

The day came for the annual family portraits, so of course Reggie was brought along to the studio. Pets were family in the Royce house. The photographer, Abe Johnson, was an old family friend and had learned years ago not to question the unusual behavior of the Royces. He set up a chair for Little Jake, who promptly fished into his pocket and pulled out a rollup cigarette and put it in his mouth before sitting down, saying "Don't want to crush it, you know, Abe? Got a light?"

Abe was unsure what to wonder about first - the fact that this toddler had a cigarette, it looked like he rolled it himself, or that he was being called by his first name by a four-year-old.

Was the problem simply that he acted like he was an adult, or was it something more? It was all too much. Maybe was time to retire. Or maybe it was time to talk to the matriarch of the Royce clan. "Being free" was a great concept until it got weird. Maybe she didn't know how "free" her great-grandchild was being raised. Could be that his parent's trust fund needed to be tightened up. Maybe they'd stop living in La-la land if they had to pay their own bills for change.

Abe always said that it did no good to children to give them a free ride in life. He was all for sparing the rod but not for spoiling child. A child with no direction and no boundaries wasn't any good to himself or anybody else.

Just as Abe released the shutter, the startled chicken released a loud squawk and an even larger splat of poop on the studio floor. Little Jake looked at the chicken, then at the horrified look on his parent's faces, and decided that this chicken thing might just work out after all.

(Originally posted 3-22-16)

Merrick's twin

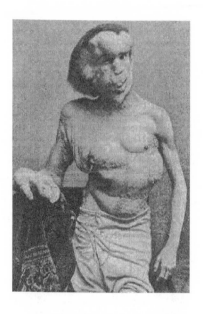

He was a monster, but only on the outside. The real monsters were those who stared at him outright, or talked about him in hushed tones as he passed. He couldn't help how he looked, but they could help how they acted - but never did. His various doctors over the years exercised cool detachment as one would expect from professionals, but then again they were under his employ. People can usually at least pretend to be nice if there is money involved.

The doctors were certain of the disease, but not so much on the cure or even the cause. They knew only the symptom but not the source. They took his money and made him feel special, but never once let on that there was no cure, only care. They could refer him to clothiers who would happily create bespoke clothing to fit his unusual frame. They knew of carpenters who could construct a bed that would allow him to sleep semi-upright to relieve the pressure on his overworked neck.

Only one person knew the true cause of his deformity, and he wanted no money for the tale. Money wouldn't cure him anyway, nothing would. John had crossed the wrong spirit one Tuesday night in October when he was 15, and he didn't even know it.

Movies were a dime on Tuesdays at the downtown three-screen theater and a quarter all other days. Even though Tuesday was a school night, John was allowed out to see the latest film once a week as long as he kept his grades above a B. Even a B- wasn't good enough and would make him lose this privilege for a whole quarter until the report cards came out again. So every other day of the week he went alone to the library to study so he could go to the movie theater on Tuesdays. Sometimes he went with friends, but he was just as likely to go by himself, savoring the peace of being out of a house with five children. Five young mouths to feed and backs to clothe meant not a lot of spare money for extravagances like movie tickets, but John had convinced his parents that he was going to be an actor when he grew up. Costly acting lessons were out of the question, so learning by watching the finished product would have to do. Even if they could have afforded private lessons, nobody in Palmyra was offering. Actors didn't move to tiny towns unless they were also close to big towns with big town amenities like airports to take them to where the jobs were. That was one reason John wanted to be an actor, to get out. Palmyra had nothing to offer anyone who was interested in something other than farming.

That fateful night he was thinking hard about how grand it would be to be an actor, where he could be himself and somebody else at the same time. It was like being a twin, he thought. He was so distracted that he tripped over the legs of Mr. Byron, the local eccentric. Mr. Byron wasn't quite homeless, and he wasn't quite crazy, but he wasn't quite much of anything that usual people liked to associate with. Most steered a wide berth around his 5-foot-eight frame, all angles and elbows. The hair on his head was jet black but it didn't mean he was young. He got his hair color from a bottle of shoe polish, having realized a decade back that actual hair dye was four times as costly. Shoe polish did the trick just the same, and he didn't mind the smell. Nobody else got close enough to notice.

Mr. Byron seemed normal when you first met him, and young ladies would take pity on him and try to befriend him. They thought that others in the town were unnecessarily rude to him, and they defended him at every opportunity. They'd make excuses for his social gaffes. This was until he turned on them, like everyone else who had gotten close. The young ladies thought he was misunderstood. In reality he was just a misanthrope.

Mr. Byron often sat on the sidewalk near the movie theater with his legs splayed out, taking up half the lane. Usually John avoided him, but this night his head was in the clouds. Later, he thought that the scrape he'd gotten on his knee from when he fell after tripping over Mr. Byron was the extent of his injuries, but he was far mistaken.

It was a month later before he noticed the change. His right side had grown heavier, thicker, denser even. His arm wouldn't stretch out like it used to. His hand started to curling in like a lobster's claw. At first he thought nothing of it. There wasn't spare money for a trip to the doctor anyway, so he did as his Mama had taught him. He drank a glass of water mixed with honey and apple cider vinegar. It was the best cure they knew and usually it worked a treat. But not this time.

Mr. Byron always worked his revenge silently. His Mama taught him that "Revenge is a dish best served cold" and boy, howdy, did he love his Mama. Whatever she taught him, directly or not, he took to heart and made it his own. All of his Mama's family had the second sight, could see right into you to know what your dreams and hopes were. Trouble was, they also knew your nightmares too. More than that, they knew how to take that raw stuff from deep in your soul and push it, shape it, like so much clay and build it up just like a mug or a vase, able to hold more than what it was before. The good ones in the family could make your dreams come true. The bad ones chose to do the same with your nightmares.

Mr. Byron was unique. He'd take your dreams, shaped them up up up, and turned them inside out, made them turn back on you so even though you got what you wished for, it wasn't ever like how you wanted.

Normally he kept to himself and didn't use his perverse talents. In years past some people would seek him out and try to get him to put a curse on another person in the town, someone who'd wronged them, either intentionally or not. At first Mr. Byron refused, but then he came to enjoy the opportunity to practice and hone his craft. Even people who do bad like to be good at it. He felt it was important that the results matched his plan. It was a sad day when something that was to go wrong didn't, or worse, turned darker and deeper than anticipated. Sometimes people needed a good scare, but ended up scarred instead. It wouldn't do to make a molehill into a mountain.

All John did that fateful night was trip over Mr. Byron's legs, so it didn't seem right what happened next. But that night was just the cherry on the sundae of slights and snubs Mr. Byron had suffered, to his mind.

John had never noticed Mr. Byron, and that was his undoing. John never said hello or good evening to him. He never asked how he was doing, inquired about Mr. Byron's family, never even invited him to see a show at the theater or out for dinner. Of course, nobody ever did any of these things, but that didn't matter to Mr. Byron, because John was the one person who crossed his path every

Tuesday night for years, so John was the focal point for his rage. There's only so much being ignored a person can take after all. Rage is like sandstone, built up tiny layer by tiny layer, week by month by year, until it is larger than a mountain and just as hard to see around.

John's dream of being an actor was turned on him that night, but it took a while before it showed. He'd been imagining how acting was like being himself and another person at the same time when he tripped over Mr. Byron. Mr. Byron caught that wish and shaped it, turned it, and made it true in the worst way possible. John became his own twin, shaped into a chimera of impossible belief. Slowly, so slowly that he didn't realize the cause and effect, he turned into a monster, half of him crabbed and lumpy, some strange cross of an ancient gnarled oak tree and a mutant crustacean. It was as if his dreamed-of other half was on stage all the time, and John was powerless to make the scene end.

(Originally posted 4-13-16)

Abraham's beard

Abraham started growing a beard just like every other boy turning into a man. His Papa taught him to shave just like his own Papa taught him. Every few days the razor came out of its leather pouch ready to do its job. In winter, when he got older, he let it grow out to keep his face warm in those biting Wisconsin winters. It didn't matter if he had an outside job that year or not, even ten minutes outside putting groceries in his car was too much cold for him. Abraham, never "Abe", had thought about moving to warmer climes many times, but that all changed when he became a monk.

His first vow was of stability - to stay right where he was and make the world right around him better instead of traveling to some far-off place where they might not speak his language or even have flush toilets. He figured that the good Lord put him here for a reason, so here was where he'd stay.

His second vow was to not cut any of his hair. Every day he washed and combed and oiled his beard and the hair in his head. This went fine until it all grew so long that he started sitting on it, or it got caught in dresser drawers. Then he started wrapping his hair up in a piece of linen, wound about and about until it was up out of the way. This worked for about a year.

After that, he started tucking his beard into his shirt pocket, just like it was a pocket watch or a handkerchief. A decade later he took to putting it over his shoulder. Sometimes he'd wear an old military jacket with a shoulder strap. It was never anything so fancy as an epaulette, just a plain piece of cloth the same color as the jacket with a button to open and close it. While the button was helpful, it had caused a snag a time or two.

The only odd thing was that Abraham was a monastery of one. Nobody else even knew he was a monk. He never dropped so much as a hint to his friends, who never would've suspected and wouldn't have believed him if he had said anything. The day after his parents died he made his vows and never swerved from them.

His third vow was to not speak about his spirituality unless he was asked. He agreed with the Lord that it was rude to brag about your holy walk, yet he also was careful not to appear as if he was denying the Lord either. It was a tight spot to be in. He figured he could tell people about his faith only if he was asked. That to him was a sign from the Lord. It was only when the traveling photographer asked him about his beard that he told, and he was the first to ask in 20 years.

Sure, people wondered about his long hair and his refusal to travel even to the next town over, but they never asked him about it. They thought that was rude to ask. That didn't prevent them from talking amongst themselves, however.

The vow of stability was a tough one. Abraham had a bear of a time getting good shoes until the Payless store opened up a franchise just three streets away from his house. His vow to stay in his town was not up for alteration. For nearly eight years he had to wear the same pair of brown Oxfords because there was no place to buy new ones - and he certainly wasn't going to buy them used. Used shirts and pants, certainly, but shoes? Never. No amount of Lysol could convince him they were clean enough. Even a monk has standards.

The city of Two Creeks, Wisconsin had never seen a traveling photographer until that bitterly cold Thursday in May. Even if it hadn't been so unusual for a photographer to appear almost overnight like a ring of mushrooms in the lawn, the cold snap would certainly have fixed the date in the minds of most of the nearly 450 people who lived there.

Abraham had walked down Zander road where his house was and turned right along Lakeshore to get to the county park. Even though it wasn't officially legal to fish there, it wasn't actually illegal either, and Abraham often took advantage of these gray areas in life. It saved him a lot of money to fish for his supper. He was just preparing his fishing lures when he heard a booming voice behind him. "Hello there, young man! Would you be interested in a free portrait of yourself this fine day?"

Abraham turned around and looked at the man for a full minute before he answered. The photographer thought that maybe he was deaf, so he began his spiel again, but Abraham held up a hand to stop him. He was trying to figure out how to answer. His first problem was being hailed as "young man" since it was as clear as the silvery hairs on his head that he was far from being a spring chicken. Either the man was trying to butter him up or he was crazy. Neither one was good.

"Why would you want to do something like that?" Abraham asked. He liked a deal, same as the next person, but he knew that "free" meant that there was a cost down the line somewhere. Nothing was ever really free, it just meant that you didn't pay for it. Someone did. That meant you were beholden, and beholden was a string. He was opposed to strings. They ended up being nooses more often than not.

The photographer explained that he worked for a national film developer who wanted to get more customers. Every person got a free 8 x 10 color glossy and eight wallet size portraits. The company figured that once folks saw how good the quality was, they'd order more. Suddenly the photographer stopped, looked at Abraham, and said "I never told anyone that before. That's the company policy, but I was given a script and trained to recite it word for word as if it were mine. Why ever did I tell you all that? Come to think of it, why am I telling you this right now? Who are you?"

And Abraham told him his story, all of it. Truth for truth, since he asked. Told him how he was a born confessor. People all over, those he knew and those he just met, told him nothing but the truth all the live long day. They felt relieved, all their guilt and shame off their chests.

It started early on, as soon as he entered kindergarten. The other children just knew and came up to him. The teachers did too. It was overwhelming at first but he got used to it – well, as much as you can get used to people telling you all their secrets. Abraham thought this was normal, because it was normal to him. He had nothing to compare it to so he never told his parents about it.

Funny thing was though, it was like a superpower. The fact that people told him all their business meant that he could handle it. It was like God gave him extra strength to be able to carry all those secrets. Maybe he didn't even carry them. Maybe it was more like he was a telephone booth, and people used him to speak to God. He figured that some people chose to dial direct, praying in their own words on their own, but then there were some who needed a person to be with them when they did it. Something about praying in an empty room made them feel like they were talking to themselves, and that bordered on crazy. Abraham was just the sort of safe person they needed.

After he told his story to the photographer, Abraham moved the very next day and left no forwarding address. It wouldn't do to let it get out that this is who he was. Soon everybody would be beating a path to his door to unburden themselves.

It was enough that people did it anyway, without even knowing that was what they were doing. It seemed honest, even pure, that way. This knowledge would turn that inside out. He might even have to set up office hours, maybe even go so far as to charge. Just the shock of thinking about the mess that would start as soon as word got out decided his mind for him.

So he shaved his beard and his head so nobody could identify him, and he started walking west, taking nothing with him. His neighbors didn't suspect a thing because he walked all the time and he never caused a fuss. It was a week later that the word of his abilities got to them, and by then his mailbox was full and the grass needed cutting. By then he had found a new life for himself and started to regrow his hair again.

(Originally posted 4-19-16)

Shoeless nuns

The Discalced Order of Carmelite nuns were barefoot, but not weak by any means. Their postulants, in addition to dressing in long plain black gowns and praying every three hours with the rest of the community, had to work out an hour every day. All that praying meant a lot of sitting, and stillness of that sort wasn't good for the body.

They looked askance at the nuns in many of the other Orders. Some of them weren't even 60 years old yet and they were obese, feeble, reduced to using a wheelchair. Worse - the wheelchairs were electric. They didn't even have to exercise their arms to get around. Just push the knob on the armrest and off they went. A Discalced Carmelite would rather renounce her vows than to be seen in such a state of sloth.

For sloth it was - a deadly sin, a sign of spiritual or emotional apathy and being physically and emotionally inactive. It was a sin because it abused the gifts of God. It was what Jesus was speaking about when he told the parable of the talents. You must take what you are given and make more of it, just like with the loaves and fishes miracle. They took seriously the adage that idle hands are the devil's playground. Inactivity invited the Accuser into the very core of the person, into the holy shrine of the soul.

The demon of sloth loved those lazy nuns especially, because he could slowly, over years, convince them to ease up on their prayers or service. He grew stronger with every forgotten prayer and every abandoned act of kindness. It would start with them thinking they could catch up later, but later never came. Only discipline kept the demon at bay. Discipline makes disciples after all. Sure, you were chosen, but you also have to choose the holy life every day, sometimes every minute. It didn't just happen.

The Carmelites never really slept. There were certainly times of rest, between prayers and work, but not many. The prayers were every three hours, and all the sisters were required to be present. Only being laid up in the infirmary was an excuse to skip. Many postulants left after just a couple of weeks of this unusual schedule, either exhausted or insane. Those who lasted soon learned what army recruits did - sleep when you can, or learn to adapt to the changed mental state that results from too little rest. Some older nuns suspected that was the goal of the frequent prayer schedule. They achieved communion with God alright - it was just not the way that was expected.

Some kept their new revelations to themselves, out of concern for being asked to leave. The Order might not take kindly to sisters with potential mental health issues. Were they really hearing from God, or was it all in their heads? Some shared their revelations only with their confessors. Some could not contain themselves, the onslaught of visions and new understanding pouring forth like water over the dam after a flood.

Those who spoke up learned that The Order was kinder than many others, and examined every revelation with respect, measuring it against scripture, tradition, and reason, to see if it was valid. They were open to the idea that God still spoke to his people.

(Originally posted 5-3-16)

Sam and the camera

Sam never felt comfortable looking people in the eye. He'd look away to the side or at his feet rather than make direct eye contact. It was too personal, too painful, like the mixing of a raw nerve in a tooth and a bit of soft bread. Out in public, his shoulders would curve inwards, trying to curl him into a ball like one of the hedgehogs he would see in his back yard. It was all about protecting the sensitive bits, for both of them. Sam wished he had spikes like they did for his first few years of life. Everything was too close, too loud, too much. It was only when he received a camera for his sixth birthday that he began to feel normal, or as normal as he thought he should.

How should he know that his senses were aberrant? It was all he knew. Abnormal was his normal, and that was all there was to it. He thought it was normal to feel like ice was in his stomach and fire in his throat every time he had to experience something different from his usual routine. He thought it was normal to feel faint from fear or anxiety for the majority of the day.

That all changed when he got the camera. The film was a 110 cartridge - easy enough for a child to install. The buttons were large and simple to use. Sam's father thought it would help him express himself, but he had no idea how helpful it was truly was.

Sam was wary of it at first, as he was of all new things, but he liked the shiny brown case and all the accessories that came with it, so soon he was using it. The strap was fun to adjust and the flash cube was enticing with its shape and sparkle. He first took pictures by holding the camera out at arm's length, not wanting to put this new thing so close to his face. After the first batch of pictures came back from the developer, his father strongly suggested he try holding the camera up to his eyes. There were simply too many wasted pictures the other way.

Something strange happened when Sam finally overcame his reluctance to put the camera to his face. Suddenly he realized he could see through the viewfinder, just as if it was a mask. He then realized that just like a mask, he was hidden from view. Suddenly his whole world opened up. Sam started taking pictures of everything and everyone. Suddenly he had a reason to go outside and be around other people. Family gatherings no longer overwhelmed him as much as before. Sure, there was still some awkwardness. That would always be there. But now he had a way to be around people that he never had before. It was like finally getting a key to unlock doors that had always been barred to him.

His father hoped that Sam would become a famous photographer, but Sam had no such ambitions. Fame was never something he wanted, at least the kind of fame he was aware of. If he could become famous without even knowing about it, then he was okay with that. He could barely handle normal human interactions. The idea of having random strangers coming up to him on the street or in the grocery store to get his autograph was enough to send him running to his room to grab his trusted teddy bear.

Fame was overrated, after all. It just meant that people were impressed that you were the best version of you there was. Meanwhile, they spent so much time focused on your achievements that they forgot to work on their own. They got jealous sometimes, forgetting that there was enough success to go around.

(Originally posted 5-14-16)

The bear story

The bear had moved in for good, and there wasn't anything Alice could do about it. Not like she wanted to, not anymore. The first week had been more difficult than she had anticipated, but after that things had slowly improved. The bear agreed, in his sure, heavy way, that this was home, this sharing a space together.

Home was never about the building. Walls and a roof didn't make a building into a home, any more than books made a library. Plenty of people have felt more at home at work in a warehouse then where they paid their mortgage. It's the people that make the difference after all.

Alice always felt that animals were more human than those who claim to be. Perhaps the utter guilelessness of them was the difference. Animals never had to prove who they were, never had to bother with such arbitrary things as status and striving. They never wore clothes, never owned cars, never had jobs. Their lives were free from all the distractions that humans had. Like children, they were given all they needed from Mother Earth and Father God. Like children, they learned at their own pace and trusted their senses. They slept when they were tired, ate when they were hungry. They never had to wonder or worry about such arbitrary and nebulous things as retirement funds or investment accounts. And as for in-laws? They never married, so that wasn't an issue.

Alice had wanted to marry the bear as soon as he moved in, but he convinced her otherwise. He reminded her that marriage is a human invention, and therefore subject to failure. If you never got married, you'll never have a risk of divorce. You are free to come and go. Doesn't it mean more if your partner stays out of love rather than obligation? Every day they stay is a gift rather than a duty.

The bear had no name as far as Alice knew. She had asked and he'd not said. He didn't talk like humans did, of course. He made his thoughts known in the way all creatures did in the beginning, with the spirit. He spoke with his whole being, resorting to sounds only as a last resort. Then they were usually snuffles and sighs and grunts. Only once had he growled, and that was when Alice had mistakenly opened a door onto his paw. After that they'd agreed to remove all of the doors inside the house. Doors just fostered separation and exclusion anyway. Plus, the knobs were hard to work with paws. The house had to work for both of them or it wouldn't work at all.

The bear didn't need a name, not really. He knew who he was. He was the only one Alice would be calling. Names meant very little when the group was small. She rarely had to call him anyway. He always knew in his slow sure way when she needed him. The same was not true for Alice, not yet. The bear often wanted to call her to look at an especially beautiful flower or sunset, but she was often so distracted by chores that she couldn't hear him call to her heart. She spent a lot of time cleaning because wanted to keep the house just so. She forgot (or never knew) that the bear didn't need to be impressed and nobody else who would come by would care.

Few people visited their home. Most of her family thought she was crazy for wanting to live with a bear. Her mother even talked about having her committed, but since she was an adult and seemed sane in all other respects, she let it drop, choosing to hold her judgment. She was prepared to shake her head and say "I told you so" while bandaging her daughter's arms from the inevitable claw marks that surely would come, but they never did. Months went by and the bear and Alice got along like peanut butter and jelly, always together, and always good. Her mother still wasn't one to concede the battle. Decades could've gone by and she still would not admit that perhaps Alice had chosen correctly. Little did she realize that Alice hadn't done the choosing. The bear had. He knew Alice needed him as much as he needed her, knew that it wouldn't be long before she'd hear him in her heart the way he heard her.

Their first meeting was as you'd expect. Bears aren't normally sought after. Normally they are run from. Alice had decided to spend a week camping by herself in the Smoky Mountains. Her job wasn't fulfilling, and she was estranged from her family in part because they felt she was wasting her talents. She decided week away to really listen was what she needed to get back on track.

Her family had paid for her college education, where she had studied veterinary science. But when she graduated and found a job at a local vet's office as an assistant, she quickly learned that what you learned in the textbooks often doesn't match with reality. It was far more visceral than she ever could have imagined. In her first week she saw more of animal's insides than their outsides.

It wasn't all physical. She'd always been a little empathic, able to feel how others were feeling even before they had words to express them. She was often able to help people before they even knew they needed it. Her friends liked her because they always felt at ease around her. She just made life easier. Meanwhile they never knew how much work this was for her.

When she was at the vet's office, she was overwhelmed with the messages of hurt and pain that she received from the animals. She had not factored in that all of them would be constantly broadcasting their hurt and confusion and pain. It was an unrelenting onslaught, since even the healthy animals that were brought in just for a check-up or a shot were anxious and confused as to what was happening to them.

When she quit after a month, her family felt she was throwing away everything she had worked for. Worse, they felt she was throwing away everything they had paid for. They refused to support her any further, so she took a job selling perfume and cosmetics at the local mall to pay her bills until she could figure out what to do next.

It was not long after that that she went on her trip. While praying for guidance late one night around the campfire, she distinctly thought she heard a voice say "Take me in". Usually she had perceived God's voice as more of a feeling than actual words, but this was crystal-clear. It was so clear that she thought that perhaps it was an actual voice, so she looked around. Just outside the glow of the fire, she saw the distinctive gleam of eyes in the shadows. They were three feet from the ground, so she knew that it wasn't an adult. She didn't realize it was a bear until he stepped forward into the firelight and stared at her, saying again "Take me in".

She ran, stumbling over tree roots and tent stakes to get away. She spent that night sleeping in the fetal position under a rhododendron bush about a mile away from her camp rather than risk being near that bear. Little did she realize but he had followed her at a slow walk, and watched over her all night as she slept to make sure that no other creature could approach her. Not all forest creatures welcomed humans into their midst.

She awoke with the dawn, stiff from rocks and roots pressing into her side. Her first thought was to give up on her quest and walk back to her car, but her keys were in her tent. She hoped that the bear hadn't savaged her camp, shredding everything in a quest for food. She'd heard stories of bears that tore through everything in a quest for sausage or Snicker's bars. The idea of rummaging through her ripped-up belongings to find her keys was not appealing, but she had no other choice.

When she finally returned she saw that everything was just as she'd left it. She had to use a hammer to re-secure the ropes from the tent pegs she'd tripped over on her midnight flight, but other than that, everything was the same. She started a small fire to cook her breakfast, and while drinking bitter coffee and eating oatmeal with blueberries she'd picked the day before, she heard the voice again. "Take me in". She looked up with a start and saw the bear, but this time he was sitting twenty feet away, staring at her. This was enough distance that she felt she didn't have to run. If she'd studied bears in college, she'd have known that no distance is a safe distance with bears. They may seem amiable and too large to run quickly, but looks are deceiving.

Alice stared at him (she assumed he was a he based on the sound of his voice in her head) and creaked out a tremulous "What?"

The bear repeated his request. "Take me in".

"What? Why? Who are you?" Alice rambled on, picking up courage. She hadn't had time to question that she was speaking with a bear. If she had, she would most likely have been silently staring at him, wondering if maybe her mind had finally cracked.

Over the course of half an hour the bear explained who he was and why he was speaking with her. He said things about being her protector, her teacher, her friend. He said he was her great-great-grandfather reincarnated. He said he had always known her and watched over her. He said that he could teach her to be the best veterinarian there ever was, or ever could be. He said that he would work with her, but first she had to let him into her life and into her heart and home.

They talked more over the course of the week she was at her campsite and worked out a plan. It was difficult for Alice to fully understand him but her natural empathic abilities went a long way. At the end of the week she went home, leaving the bear there, but she promised to return.

She quit her meaningless job as soon as she returned, not even bothering to go in to turn in her notice. She called the assistant manager at 7 on a Tuesday morning, waking him from his hangover from his one-person-party the night before. She told him that she had quit, and that was that. She hung up as he stuttered his questions at her, not believing. He'd never listened anyway.

She sold everything she had to make enough money to move to the woods and build a small cabin there for her and the bear. It was fortunate that she didn't need much, because she didn't have much. She traded out for much of what she needed by going to the Goodwill. Her worldly possessions transformed from frilly dresses to sturdy cotton clothes, the better to work in. Her CD collection became an axe and a saw so she could cut down trees to make a home.

The bear worked with her, pushing trees down, dragging logs over, lifting them up. After a month they were both tired but there was a roof over their heads. They had no furniture but they didn't care. The work was so exhausting that they didn't need a fluffy bed to rest in. They both slept deeply, curled up on the earthen floor of their new home, the bear curled protectively around Alice. She loved the musky, earthy smell of his fur and how it was somehow soft yet bristly at the same time. At times she could smell pine sap and warm summer sun in his fur, traces of his adventures while away from her.

They spent much time working together, he teaching her about all the ways of the animals. He filled in all of the knowledge she'd missed in her classes. He introduced her to all the animals in the forest and taught her how to speak with them – but more importantly how to listen. He told her that she didn't have to wonder what was wrong when they came to her – they would tell her if she asked.

Yet still there was a wall between them. She had learned the language of the birds and the deer, of all the animals that flew or walked or slithered. Yet she was never fully able to hear the bear, not as well as the other animals. Perhaps he was too different, too tame. Perhaps he'd given up part of his wildness for his ability to live with her. Perhaps there was still too much of his human spirit in him, buried deep down in his bear heart, for her to hear him like she could hear others. He wasn't quite a bear, yet he wasn't quite a person, but both, and neither, and something more.

(Originally posted 5-19-16)

Dolly dearest

After nearly 5 years, Sara's dolly had started to talk. Sure, Sara talked to it, dressed it, gave it a name. She even pretended to feed it cookies and tea every Sunday afternoon. She'd even thought she'd heard it answer her before, but it was always in her head or her heart. It was never out loud.

The first time she heard it out loud she thought she was imagining it. The second time, just a moment later, she thought her older sister Janey was playing a trick on her, throwing her voice. It was just like her to torment her little sister in ways that she could easily deny later to their busy and no-nonsense parents. Sara had learned early on that if she brought up charges, there had better be proof or the punishment she expected Janey to get would fall on her. She'd also learned that it was best to settle matters herself right away.

Sara jumped up off the bed, scattering her coloring pages and crayons and scrambled to her bedroom door. She jerked back the door, expecting to see her sister's back as she ran away. But nobody was there. The hall was empty - not even the sound of bare feet dashing away. Stunned, Sara went to find her sister. After a few minutes she found her outside on the hammock reading some book with dragons on the cover. There was no way Janey could have gotten there that fast. Sara slowly walked back to her room via the kitchen, helping herself to a piece of banana bread and a glass of lime Kool-Aid. She did all her best thinking when she had a snack.

As soon as she sat down on her bed, with her dolly nestled in her lap, she heard it speak again.

"Won't you give me some of your snack?"

The voice was so soft and so sad, so full of loss and longing. Sara held the doll out at arm's length and stared at it, blinked her eyes. Then, with slow horror, she watched her doll blink her eyes too.

"You're always pretending to feed me, but you never do. You're such a tease. No wonder nobody plays with you."

Sara was frozen with fear, yet managed to stammer out "How can you talk?"

Her dolly said "Silly! How do you think anybody learns how to talk? I listened. I listened to you blabbering on about how sad you are. I listened to your sister taunt you about being a scaredy-cat. I listened to your parents fight. I've listened to all of it. I've listened to the television announcers talk about pollution and war. I've heard the songs on the radio about getting even and how things were better back then. All I ever hear is sad sad sad, so that's who I am. I'm everything you've ever cried about, because you've never shared your good days with me. My hair is matted from your tears. What did you expect? You made me this way."

Sara threw her doll into the middle of the room and retreated to the furthest corner, curled up into a ball. It was nearly half an hour later before she realized her mistake - the doll was between her and the door. How could she escape? She put off the decision a little while longer, but soon she realized she had to pee and there was no ignoring that. It was either creep past that accursed doll or go here in the corner. Even though she was young, she knew that would be a bad idea. Even if her Mom didn't find out soon and punish her for it, Sara would smell the sickly sweet smell of her dried urine whenever she was in her room. Going to sleep would be terrible. She had to risk it.

Keeping her eyes on the doll, she slowly got up so as not to startle it. As slow as a cat stalking a cricket, she moved around the edge of the room as far away from her former best friend and confidant as she could.

She had told it everything. All the things she couldn't say out loud to her Mom, her sister, her friends, she told the doll. All her fears, all her failings. Every little sneaky thing she'd done to get back at her sister without her knowing. She'd poured all of her darkness into this doll, and none of her joy.

The slow realization of what this meant descended upon her like an evening fog, clouding her vision, narrowing it to a pinpoint. She knew with dreadful certainty what she had to do next. She must destroy the doll.

So far, there was no movement from the accursed thing, but she couldn't be sure this would continue. She'd thought it would stay silent for all those years, but that had changed. What other horrible changes would happen? Just because it wasn't moving now didn't mean it wouldn't start, and soon. She had to destroy it as quickly as possible before it ruined her life.

She closed the bedroom door behind her and dragged a chair from her sister's room to jam up under the doorknob. That would buy her some time to think of her plan. She almost forgot her need to use the bathroom in her fright, but she took care of that now. While in the calm and quiet space of the hall bathroom, she considered her options.

Burial wasn't good. Her Mama would get mad about the mess she'd make, and how could she be sure the doll would stay buried? It might dig itself out. Perhaps she should chop it up first. Then she realized if she did that she could put all the pieces in separate places around town. The head could go under the drainpipe of the neighbor's house at the end of the block, an arm in the trashcan in her school's bathroom. There's no way it could reassemble itself then. But maybe the head could still talk, she realized with a cold shudder. She'd better bury it, at least, to be sure.

Burning it was right out. Her Mama would whip her if she caught her playing with matches again. She'd gotten in trouble for that when she was three, having set a flip-flop on fire, wanting to see how the rubber melted. It melted alright, and so did the carpet it was on, and the curtains, and the entire bedroom. The whole family had to stay in a motel room for nearly 4 months until the insurance company got the restoration work done. While it was an adventure for the girls, it was a headache for the parents, so they made sure that Sara understood they were not kidding about fire safety. Janey used it as yet another way to torment her little sister, who she never wanted in the first place. Anything she could do to get her to leave her alone, or even leave, was fair game.

This was proving to be the hardest thing Sara had had to contend with in all her tender years. Maybe she could preempt the doll and confess all her slights and sins to her mother before the doll did. Just thinking about that made her stomach go icy cold and wobbly. There were a lot of things to confess.

You or I would consider them trivial, but

Sara, with her limited experience, thought them worthy of eternal damnation. The perspective that comes with time downgrades childhood sins to summer showers instead of the tornadoes that they seem to be at the time. She had plenty of time to learn what real sins were about, but as for now, she felt damned.

But she didn't have plenty of time to figure out what to do about the doll. So she did what she was taught to do in Sunday school. Not like she did a lot, but she figured it couldn't hurt to try.

"God?" She murmured, on her knees on the cold porcelain tile on the bathroom floor, "I could use some help right now, if you're not too busy and all."

Sara wasn't sure she had a good connection, because she couldn't hear God's reply. Was praying like talking on the telephone? Sometimes when she was talking to her grandmother in Canada the connection wasn't that good. Also, often Gram's hearing wasn't that good either. Her mother always told her to keep on talking anyway, that Gram could make it out. Maybe God was the same way? It was worth a try. It wasn't like she had anybody else she could call. This was some big stuff. She needed to go straight to the top.

"God? I hope you can hear me because I sure need some help here."

Sara heard a voice so quiet that she ignored it at first. It was centered in the middle of her chest, about heart high, and not in her ears. She didn't hear it so much as feel it. The feeling-voice said to do nothing at all, to not destroy the doll, to not say anything at all to her parents about it. To act as if everything was normal. This seemed too easy, she thought, but precisely because it made no sense she decided it might actually be a message from God. She would never have come up with this on her own. And, if nothing else, it required almost no effort on her part. It was going to be difficult to pretend everything was fine when it most certainly wasn't, but if God insisted, there must be a good reason. She decided to play along.

The doll said nothing the next day or the next one after that. It was nearly a full week later before it spoke again, and this time it was around Sara's Mom. She was straightening up Sara's room one morning and the doll suddenly started to talk, as clear as you please, staring straight at her. Sara's Mom stopped making the bed and stood stock-still, refusing to turn and face the voice. It sounded just like her mother, who had been dead for 18 years, long before her children were born. In fact, she realized suddenly with a guilty shudder, the anniversary of her death had been two weeks ago and she had forgotten.

She usually remembered, usually dreaded that day. Her mother had been the model of motherhood in public - PTA chair, Girl Scout troop leader. She even had started her own nonprofit tutoring business to teach all the recent influx of immigrant children and their parents how to read and write in English. Three times in her life she had gotten the coveted "Citizen of Lewisburg" award given out at a huge gala once a year.

Only Laurie, Sarah's mom, knew the truth. Only she knew the true evil that lay beneath the façade that everyone else saw. Only she knew how twisted and damaged her mother was, yet because everyone else saw her as a saint, nobody believed her when she asked for help. She tried to tell her teachers about the emotional and mental abuse she suffered from her but they never listened for long, thinking Laurie was making up a story. "You're so creative!" they'd exclaim, and encourage her to write for the fiction column in the school newspaper. "But try to write something nicer next time, honey. Girls don't write scary stories, do they?" they'd suggest.

After a while, Laurie chose to be silent about the abuse. Her mother was clever. It never was physical. There never were bruises or scrapes. Even if there had been nobody would have believed her anyway.

She didn't dare look at the doll, but she didn't dare turn her back to it either. It kept speaking, kept taunting her. It had chosen well. Nobody else was home. Nobody else could listen in. She could keep digging in, taking up where she left off 18 years ago. Laurie was deer in the headlights frozen, speechless. For the longest time the doll kept talking and Laurie listened, breathless, immobile. After an eternity, the shallow breaths she had been unconsciously taking caught up with her and she suddenly drew in a huge breath to make up. It was then that she recovered her power.

Without a word, she snatched up the doll by its arm from the corner chair it was in and carried it to the nearest trashcan. Without a word she swept up the handles of the brown plastic Kroger bag she used as a trashcan liner and tied them shut. Without a word she scooped up the rest of the trash in the house, put it all together in a huge black bag her husband kept for cleaning up after yardwork, snatched her car keys that were hanging from the hook by the front door and marched straight out to her car. Within 10 minutes she was at the city dump and the deed was done.

She was still shaking by the time she got back home. After a little internal debate, she decided to go for a quick walk around the neighborhood first and then have some linden tea. Yes. That order seemed best. Time to shake out some energy and then brush away the crumbs.

Sara got home from school and went straight to the kitchen for a snack. She took her gingersnaps and lemonade to the porch to enjoy. Normally she would go straight to her room to share it with her dolly, but after it had started to talk she had changed her ways. She spent as little time in her room as possible now. She couldn't bear to think of it staring at her while she slept. She was sure her teddy bear and stuffed giraffe could protect her from it, but she didn't want to risk them being harmed in the fight. Plus it wasn't fair to ask a doll to fight against another doll. It was against their code, after all.

But then she soon remembered that she planned to color after school today, and her crayons were in her room. There was nothing for it except to do it, so she got up and went to her room. Waiting was only going to increase her dread and make it harder. Best to get it over with.

In the past week she had learned to not look in the corner chair where she had put her dolly after that terrible day. So she almost missed that it wasn't there. A wave of terror like ice water poured over her when she noticed its absence. Where was it? Had it finally started to walk? Had it talked to her Mom and told her everything and she was now going to be interrogated?

Sara remembered the still small voice she'd heard when she prayed for guidance a week ago. Don't worry about it, act like everything is fine, it said. So she pulled herself together and gathered up her crayons and coloring books and went back to the porch. By then her Mom was there sipping her tea. Their eyes met and both smiled awkward, guarded smiles. Something passed between them - a truce? An understanding? For the rest of their lives they never talked about the missing doll.

(Originally posted 7-12-16)

Molly under cover

The Eames children could not bear to be without their mother. Simply losing sight of her would set one, and then all of the children to wailing. Even after she returned to the room it took a good ten minutes to assuage them.

It was a worrisome thing. You'd expect it from babies. They are so helpless. Their every need has to be taken care of by an adult, and often that was their mother. It stood to reason they'd think she was God. Plenty of adults acted the same way, come to think of it. When everything started to go sideways they forgot themselves and made it worse with all their worrying.

Perhaps it was because the children were so close in age that it kept happening, the self-reinforcing feedback loop. The boys were only a year apart. For Molly Eames it felt like she was pregnant two years running. She had no intention to make it three so she simply told Mr. Eames that there would be no sex for year (at least) until she felt like going through that ordeal again.

She'd not expected marriage to be like this. Her mother, either out of modesty or meanness, never told her where babies came from, or more accurately how they got there in the first place. She was horrified to learn the secret and was incredulous at first. How was that even possible? Much of her life was a mystery to her. Her parents were conservative on many fronts and had homeschooled her to keep her from being "infected by the disease of the world" as they so often informed her. It was for her own good, they said. It was like she was a time capsule, a frozen moment in a fictional time when everything was safe. Their greatest hope was that she'd be a beacon of light in the dark times they knew were soon to come.

Her lack of education chafed at her once she realized it. If she could get pregnant from contact with a part of her husband's body, then what else could happen? What else had been hidden from her? After her first check up at the obstetrician she went straight to the library and got every book they had on biology. Three weeks later she returned them all and decided to start at the beginning of the nonfiction section and work her way through the entire collection.

She told no one in her family what she was doing, least of whom her husband. She even made sure to confirm that her library record was private when she got her card. She figured if her family had hidden important knowledge from her then they must think she wasn't worthy of it, or that it wasn't worth their time to tell her. So she decided it wasn't worth her time to tell them otherwise.

Molly Eames couldn't hold off from sex indefinitely, however. Her husband was becoming insufferable, acting as if he was a prisoner of war in his own home. If he'd had to endure what she had - months of nausea, clothes not fitting, and even swelling in fingers and feet (not to mention the painful and embarrassing ordeal of actually giving birth) he might have thought differently about sex. Ten minutes of fun wasn't worth nine months of feeling possessed by an alien being.

Giving birth was the most difficult thing Molly had ever been through. It wasn't joyful at all. She simply didn't understand the chittering from her neighbors and friends who gushed about how wonderful it all was. Maybe they were lying. Maybe they were insane. Maybe the whole experience had turned them permanently crazy with no hope of recovery. The worst part wasn't even the pain, which was so bad it created a whole new category of suffering. It became her new ten on the pain chart, a place formerly occupied by having her arm set without anesthesia at 12 after she fell out of a tree.

She never climbed a tree again after that. Just like with sex, the risk wasn't worth the fun. It's not like her husband was any good at it anyway. He called it "making love", never "having sex" but it wasn't lovely at all. It was sweaty and awkward and strange. Perhaps other people were used to being naked in front of others, but Molly wasn't. There was nothing exciting about it. She was always trying to cover up with the sheets. She wasn't trying to hide how she looked so much as not be cold. Her husband wasn't much to look at either, and he only took a bath once a week, and then only if she insisted.

The "being naked" part of being an adult was a great shock. Her parts most certainly weren't private when she had to go for her checkups when she was pregnant but at least that was just the doctor who saw. When she gave birth, it seemed like the whole hospital was staring at her nether regions. She briefly considered selling tickets to offset the bill.

Even though her two children were very clingy, she had agreed to produce three when they had that discussion before marriage. It was important to work out such things. Children or not, standard of living expected, minimum expectations of signs of affection - all of these needed to be negotiated before you said "I do". Too many folks didn't see marriage as the legal contract that it was, hoping love would right all wrongs and mend all wounds. Without clear agreements it caused more trouble than it cured.

But she'd promised three, so three it must be. There was nothing to it except to do it, so she determined her most fertile time from some of the research she had done and had sex once more to provide her end of the contract. Better get it out of the way, like ripping a Band-Aid off. To prolong the suffering was pointless.

Walter Eames wanted a picture of the children, but not of his wife. He was sick of who she had become - no longer meek or mild. She seemed more confident, more aware. She certainly wasn't the person he had married - someone he could push around all day long with nary a peep. Not like he thought he was pushy, no, never. Being assertive and decisive had gotten him to where he was at work, but it was getting him nowhere at home. Debate and compromise weren't part of his repertoire.

But there was no way to photograph them without her. The moment she would walk away from them, they'd set up a wail worse than a tornado siren. It was ridiculous. She couldn't even go to the bathroom without them pitching a fit. It was embarrassing to go out in public with his family, so he didn't. Far from being a source of pride as he had expected before he got married, he now frequently left them at home and went out by himself. Even though he'd worked all day and she stayed home with the children (that one attempt at day care changed any plans they might have had of her working outside of the home), he was happy to spend even more time away. This was not turning out to be the life he'd planned as an adult.

So when it came time to get a portrait made, he had to get creative. His parents had asked to see the kids for years. He refused to make the six hour drive with her, and his parents were too frail to make the drive themselves. A portrait would have to do. He looked around the studio and his eyes landed on a backdrop. "That'll do!" he exclaimed, and snatching it up, pushed his wife into the chair, dropped the fabric over her, arranged the kids around her, and ordered the photographer to snap away. Other than the sound of the shutter release, the room was silent. Nobody other than him could believe this was happening.

(Originally posted 7-20-16)

Ella

Ella had been raised with humans since she was a wee calf, only two months old. She'd been abandoned by her mother, who simply walked away one afternoon while Ella was sleeping in the damp savannah heat under a baobab tree.

Perhaps the mother forgot her? Perhaps she walked off to check on a strange sound or find something to eat. Perhaps she didn't want to be a mother anymore. Perhaps she was too young for the experience, or it was more than she'd anticipated.

Regardless of the reasons why, the "what" was that Ella was by herself for a day and a night before she was found by a safari full of New Zealand tourists. That area wasn't on their tour, but her bellows aroused their curiosity so they rerouted.

Ella was fine for a few hours after she awoke. It wasn't unusual for Mama to go away. Calves had to learn to be independent early on, so mothers didn't coddle them. But when sunset came and Mama still wasn't there she started to get a little anxious. That hungry feeling in her tummy got more insistent, which only worsened her anxiety. It was a terrible self-reinforcing loop.

Ella began to whine, quietly at first, feeling sad and alone. She didn't want to call the wrong sort of attention to herself. There were plenty of animals in the Savannah who would love to make a meal of a young elephant left unguarded by her parents. But after a few hours alone under the stars, Ella started the bawl openly, no longer holding back. She no longer cared if some predatory animal was drawn to her cries. Death was better than this, this half-life of loneliness and fear.

What would she do? How would she care for herself? Her Mama had been her world, her constant companion. And now as far as she looked across the flat scrubland, she saw nothing but thorn bushes and trees stripped of their leaves by the giraffes. She was still awake, red-eyed and hoarse from her keening in the early morning when the safari group found her.

A young couple, Mr. and Mrs. Jacob Halverson, married just 6 1/2 months, decided to take her as their own. They'd agreed when they were engaged that they didn't want children, both having been raised by abusive parents. They didn't trust themselves to not repeat the pattern. It was as if they both chosen to be teetotalers after being raised by alcoholics. They decided it was safer for everyone all around if they didn't even try. But an elephant was another matter entirely. And who couldn't fail to fall in love with her? Her huge dark eyes with her long ashes locked into them like a tractor beam. There was no chance of escape.

However, there were a few obstacles to overcome. How to get her home? An airplane was out of the question. If airlines charge by the pound for luggage, there's no way they can get her on board. Perhaps a combination of train and boat? It was the only way it seemed. However, the moment they put her on the train for the first time they knew there was going to be a problem. She began to bawl when Jake stepped out of the car. He and Margie quickly realized one of them would have to stay with her.

They hurried to get another ticket and had to pay extra for the "privilege" of riding in the animal car. It wasn't meant for people, and Mr. Gruber, the engineer, had to pay off the station manager to keep him from grumbling. Fortunately the weather was good, because the animal cars weren't air-conditioned. No use wasting heat and air on them, the company thought. But Jacob would have a hard time. Even though it was early summer, the speed of the train would mean it would be rather chilly while it was traveling. Margie gave him her mink coat that he'd given her as an engagement gift to soften the blow. The other animals kept away from him once they caught a whiff of it, unsure of what it, or he, was. It masked his aftershave, however, and that was good. He was grudgingly accepted as one of them at least long enough to get Ella to her new home.

(Originally posted 2-14-17)

The Clower twins

Emma hated her siblings. All day long she had to rock them back and forth. Even if they'd had arms and legs they were too small to do it themselves. Rocking was the only way to keep them content, but more importantly, to keep them quiet. Her shoulder was getting tired, but she kept at it. To stop meant noise either from them or from their parents. Or both. She wasn't sure which was worse, but she was unwilling to learn the answer right now.

The twins were born three years ago but they looked half that age. They were so tiny, still. The doctor in Millersville was unable to tell Mr. and Mrs. Clower if they would always be this small, or if they would ever catch up. He also had no answer to why they had no arms or legs. He didn't have a lot of answers for most of their questions, but he was all they had. They couldn't afford to take the twins into Baltimore to get a second opinion. It was only 22 miles away, but that was forever when you didn't have a car. Sure, it was only two hours by bicycle, but those babies couldn't travel that way, no sir! How would they take them - in the basket like they were a package to be mailed or a bag of apples bought at the market? You can't hold them and steer, either. Plus it would mean that Earl had no way to get to his job at the field, picking beans or tending the goats. No, one opinion would have to do, even though it wasn't much. If the good Lord had wanted them to know more, He would've provided more. This was their burden, and they had to carry it.

Now, to be sure, Mr. and Mrs. Clower never said out loud that their newest children were a burden. They never intentionally sounded ungrateful for any gift the Lord gave them, no matter how odd it seemed. Their pastor had said years ago that nothing from the Lord was bad, only it might be bitter sometimes. Medicine was bitter, but it was good for you. And it took a while to see the effects. They remembered his words when the twins came, and thought about them often.

Why, the Lord Himself was born in a barn. That sure didn't seem appropriate for God to make an appearance. Surely God would be born in a palace or at least a manor house. Never someplace so anonymous or dirty as a pen for animals. Imagine the noise! Imagine the smell! So if the Lord could be born in less than ideal circumstances, so could their babies. They'd just have to wait and see how things turned out, just like Mary did.

Emma didn't have the patience to wait. She wanted these babies gone and she wanted them gone right now. They were getting on her nerves. She hadn't asked to be a big sister. She had been fine being an only child. She sure didn't want the limelight taken away from her, and even more she didn't want to have to care for these interlopers.

Her parents never thought twice about making her tend them. It was part of her job as a member of the family. They didn't charge her rent or expect her to pay for her food or clothing, so how else was she supposed to do her part? The same had been expected of them, both first-borns in large families. Of course you needed large families then. It was free labor. Having children was like printing money. Need more help? Have more babies. Of course you had to plan ahead a bit - look down the road a piece in order to see what you might have need for. It didn't do to have a baby right when times got tight - then you were doubling your trouble. Best to have one who was at least five, so he was able to feed and clothe himself. It didn't count as child labor if it was yours, you know.

But these babies weren't going to be a help to anyone, seeing as how they were born without limbs. They sure were happy, though. That made it a little easier. All day long they laughed and smiled, eyes gleaming at everyone and everything. Some thought they were soft in the head, being so happy and all. It takes smarts to see the troubles in the world. But they really were smart and happy at the same time. It was weird. Maybe that was their gift. They'd been cursed physically, but blessed spiritually. They were happy no matter what was happening, which was good. Now, if only they could rub off some of that spirit onto Emma.

(Originally posted 4-21-17)

Bone music

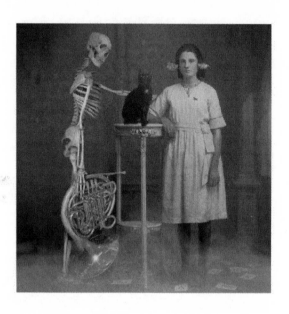

Harold loved playing the French horn. The tone was mellow and warm, inviting. He knew it would never be the lead instrument like the trumpet or guitar was, and he was fine with that. He wasn't one for being in front, leading the way. No, that was for the peacocks in the world. He was more a pigeon, behind-the-scenes, anonymous. He never wanted to be a manager, bossing people around. He was happy being a team member, a cog in the wheel, someone who got things done without any fanfare.

And then he met Lydia. She loved him exactly the way he was, for who he was. She wasn't put off by his meek nature or unassuming presence. She certainly wasn't concerned that he was a skeleton, either. While most women were loathe to live with someone who looked like they escaped from an anatomy class, Lydia saw the advantages. Because he had no skin, he was never too hot or too cold. She could adjust the thermostat to whatever she liked and he'd never fuss. He never spent any money on clothes either, so they had plenty set aside to go on vacations.

And go on vacations they did! Every month they ventured to a new part the world, seeing a new place and meeting new people. They picked their destinations from their extensive list of pen-pals, strewn all over the globe like Easter eggs, each one a treasure to discover. Every year they had to get new passports made because they'd filled them up with stamps and visas. Lydia had a plan that the old pages could be used to re-wallpaper her art room one day.

Mr. Buttons, their cat, never got to go on a trip. He never left the house. The vet even came to him. He was terrified of the outside world. Trees sent him into a tizzy. Clouds? Forget about it. He'd run and hide under Lydia's dress, cowering there until she picked him up and carried him back inside. Otherwise he'd stay there, trembling, paralyzed. It was kind of embarrassing really, but it did mean that they never had to worry about him sneaking out when they opened the door, or be bothered with him asking to go out and come back in every 15 minutes. No, all in all he was a good cat, and he seemed to enjoy Harold's home recitals almost as much as Lydia did.

They met at one of his performances - that time in a mutual friend's house. Jane had suspected they'd get along smashingly and set up the recital as an excuse for them to meet. It was the blindest of blind dates - neither one knew that they were being steered toward each other. Harold brought his French horn and Lydia brought her harmonica. While listening to the sousaphonist playing his solo, (a piece he wrote himself for the occasion) they began to talk.

Lydia was certain that she'd heard undertones in Harold's playing - notes that she was uniquely capable of hearing because of her unusual ears. Nobody in her family talked about her ears, but she knew she was different. She assumed they didn't want to talk about them out of kindness, to not make her feel different, or perhaps it was out of embarrassment. Nobody really was certain who her father was, after all. Sure there was a man who filled the role, who was married to her mother. Jack had raised her since she was a baby. Everybody knew he was Dad and not her Father.

The only person who knew for sure was Martha, Lydia's Mom, and she wasn't saying. She'd retired from the circus when she got pregnant and that was as far as the story went. Sure, there had been a mule act as part of the show, but nobody went so far as to suggest anything that questionable. Maybe it was the illusionist, spurned at the end, and he performed some real magic instead of those sleight-of-hand stunts that were his bread-and-butter. No matter, the family didn't know and it wasn't worth the bother of making up a story, so they just acted like everything was normal.

Harold said that yes, he regularly played more notes then were normally heard, basically playing two songs at once. If it was a depressing song, he simultaneously played a cheery one at a subsonic level to even it out. If it was a rousing march, he played a dirge for the same reason. He just felt it wasn't right to bring people's emotions too high or too low. Somewhere in the middle was best, and since he could, he did.

Nobody before had discovered the extra song weaving its way into and under the first, like how the framework of the house is hidden yet integral to the house itself. Nobody until now, he thought, and there and then he decided he would have to make her his bride. Partly it was out of admiration for her rare talent. But partly it was out of the desire to keep his actions a secret. No wife could testify against her husband - that was law. It was like testifying against yourself since "the two shall be of one flesh". It stood to reason she wouldn't tattle on him either, as a logical extension of that law.

She hadn't told, and he never had reason to worry. She wouldn't have anyway. Nobody ever believed her when she told them anything she'd learned from using her unusual talent. They had no way to check if it was true, and honestly they didn't care. In some ways she was like a five-year-old boy, fascinated with trains or dinosaurs, telling everyone within earshot about the minutest details of her obsession. Even though what Lydia said was true it didn't really concern them, so it wasn't worth the bother. "Uh-huh!" and "Is that right?" they'd mumble to not appear rude, but they were already off thinking about their own interests. She never took it personally, knowing their actions said more about them than her, and learned to keep her own counsel early on.

(Originally posted 4-21-17)

Lost and Found Penguin

Sara thought Petey was her brother, and nobody had the heart to tell her otherwise. They'd grown up together, after all. Sarah and her mom had found him hopping on the shoreline near their home in Athenree, New Zealand. Rockhoppers were all over the coast, but it was rare for one to venture into Shelly Bay.

They left him where he was, and her mom promised that they would check on him the very next day. The toddler wanted to take him home right then but her mom said they didn't have anything for him to eat. Sara didn't think that was a good enough reason because she knew the Four Square market was open. Mama had to admit she was worried that he might be lost and looking for his family. She hadn't wanted to say that, not knowing how Sara would take it. Would she feel for him, be sad that he was alone, and then insist on adopting him right away? This was not a situation she wanted to deal with on a Tuesday afternoon. She just wanted to go on a wander with her daughter and then come home to afternoon tea and a nap, preferably in that order.

Sara was concerned, but not overly so, and Mama again assured her they'd come back tomorrow and check on him. She hoped that he'd be gone and forgotten by then. Children have such short memories, and sometimes that was a blessing.

The rest of the day passed uneventfully. Mama had forgotten about the little lone penguin by the next afternoon. But he hadn't forgotten about them. As soon as she opened the garage door to leave for their daily walk, he was standing there in the side yard. Sara shrieked with delight and started to run towards him. She hadn't forgotten about him at all. Mama called to her to stay away but it was too late. She was already embracing him in a full-on hug as only a toddler can. It was a hug that was a bit like a tackle and a lot like a reunion after a wartime deployment. Fortunately the penguin seemed to be just as enthusiastic, flapping his stubby wings and chirruping in high-pitched squeals. You would have thought they were long-lost friends if they were of the same species.

Mama stood there in amazement, taking in the scene. Maybe he had followed them home? They lived not far from the shoreline, and there weren't any roads he (Mama assumed it was a he - how do you to tell?) would have had to cross. How long had he been there? Sara's voice broke through her musings.

"Mama he's here! Our Petey!" she exclaimed in delight, her face lighting up like the sun.

"Sara, sweetheart, we can't keep him, he's a wild animal. There are laws about this." She wasn't certain about this but it sounded very parental to say. "And Petey? Is that his name?" - knowing that naming a pet meant it was harder to get rid of it. Name it and keep it.

Anonymous animals came and went, but named ones stayed. How did she come up with Petey? They didn't have any friends or relations named that. It wasn't out of any picture book they'd gotten from the library to read at bedtime.

"He told me his name was Petey!" Sara beamed, and she hugged him all the more. He seemed a little overwhelmed and on the verge of being smothered by this point, but overall still quite happy to be found. Mama wondered if Sara could translate his squeaks and chitters. "How did he tell you, baby?" She used her most reasonable voice now. This wasn't in her plans. Daniel would be upset when he came back from his business trip tomorrow to discover they had adopted a penguin. Or a penguin had adopted them. She wasn't sure.

"He told me in my heart," Sara said, and letting go of her newfound best friend with one hand, she placed it over her heart to show her mom. Sometimes she had to point things out to her mom to make sure she understood. Even toddlers know that parents can be a little dense sometimes.

Sara's mom wasn't sure how to take this. Was her daughter making things up again? Or was this a sign of a mental illness? It was hard to separate the two sometimes. Was this why so many artists and writers went off the deep end? This wasn't going so well. She was supposed to be the adult, after all, supposed to be in charge. Toddlers weren't supposed to run the show, although they often did. Adults just thought they were in control. Meanwhile, toddlers determined when and if they slept, and where and how they ate. The fact that Sara was an only child amplified her power over her parents.

It was not long before Petey became a member of the family. He lived outside, however, so he wasn't a full member. Mama thought it was safer all around to not bring him inside, and the weather was always mild where they lived. She was concerned that if they brought him in they'd have to notify the animal control department. But if he lived outside, they could still think of him as "wild" and he could come and go as he wished. If they brought him in there might be shots and laws to be considered. Plus, there was always the thought that it wasn't fair to keep him in. Daniel, once he got home and was consulted, remembered a roommate he'd had in college who'd kept a bird in a cage as a pet. He'd always thought there was something cruel and vain about that, because birds aren't meant to live inside like dogs or cats. They are meant to be free. Penguins were birds too, after all.

Sara's parents started to think of Petey as their second child, and while they never said that out loud to friends or coworkers, they were never so bizarre as to refer to him as their "featherbaby". He was an animal, a quasi-pet. They loved him, but he wasn't human.

Except to Sara. She remained the only child that Mr. and Mrs. Fullerton had, so she didn't know any different. To her, Petey was her younger brother. It didn't matter to her that he never learned how to speak English and never went to school. She understood that he was a little different than her friend's siblings, and she was OK with that. All of her childhood she looked forward to going home after school and getting to see her best friend, who still waddled about in the back yard, still pleased as punch to see her.

(Originally posted 5-17-17)

The Wooden Dolly

Maybelle was a bad doll, but she couldn't help it. The wood that she'd been carved from was terribly damaged. Only one person knew that, and he wasn't telling. He couldn't. He was dead. The act of creating her had been the last thing he did. He hadn't planned it that way.

Drogon was the village doctor - medical and otherwise. If you were out of sorts, you went to Drogon. Before that you'd have gone to Drogon's father, and now you'd have to go to Drogon's son, even though he was only seven. These kinds of doctors didn't get trained in schools, or even by their parents. There was no apprenticeship. The moment the father breathed his last, his spirit and everything he'd learned traveled into the son. It had gone on so long that everybody in the village accepted it as normal, just like how flowers came out in the spring and leaves went away in the fall. The village was many miles from any other so the residents had no way of knowing this was unusual. It was only in the past decade that they'd even learned they weren't the only people in this country, or even on the planet.

They'd never ventured any further than a few feet from "the edge of the world" as they called it. Why would they? Everything they needed was here. Exploration comes from want and need. If you have everything you want or need, you don't tend to go exploring. Art was created for the same reason - out of a sense of lack and loss. Folks who felt content weren't artists. Artists were forever plagued to create even more art, because what they made never felt quite right to them. The fact that they had a sense of something missing in the world caused them to make art – but then still feel incomplete.

Drogon was an artist as well as a doctor - never satisfied with his work. He was certain he could do better with his healing. This was unlikely, since he'd inherited 16 generations worth of healing knowledge when his father died. Everything his father had learned had passed on to him, as it had happened to himself when Drogon's grandfather had died. It was an amazing process. One day you were yourself, the next you had all these voices in your head giving you unsolicited advice on what to do. It was a little like a family reunion but only one person heard the jokes, and thankfully nobody brought the green bean casserole.

Not many years after their first visit from the outside (as everything other than the village was called), Drogon had a visitor from very far away. He was told that everyone there spoke a different language than him and thought differently, acted differently, dressed differently. He was told that they weren't as clever as the villagers, because they couldn't make up stories to entertain themselves in the evenings. He was shocked to learn that hundreds of people would even pay to sit and listen to a person entertain them, to tell them stories, even hearing stories through the air on something called television, rather than in person. Drogon thought that there must be a huge drought on stories there to have to go to that extreme.

This visitor wanted Drogon to make her a very special doll - one that could tell stories to her people. She'd had a successful career as a ventriloquist, but this would be different. This would be special. This would be so amazing that she could retire early, at the top of her game. She wouldn't have to suffer the indignity of having to do ads for life insurance or hearing aids in her later years, as so many of her fellow performers did. She wouldn't have to hawk (or hock) anything. She'd be set, if only he would make this new dummy with some of his magic. She told him nothing of her own needs - only that he would be helping her people with their story-sickness.

Drogon had assured her that he had no such skill, no ability to make wood talk, but she was persistent, and he soon felt sorry for these people so far away who had to pay someone to do something they could do for themselves. He promised nothing, but said he would try. That night, he did something he'd never done before - he called a family conference.

That night, he called together all 16 generations of healers from his family. Never before had Drogon even attempted to rouse them. Normally they were just there in his head when he needed them. But this was different. This was a sickness as sure as malaria, as certain as cholera. To be without stories was a sickness of the soul, a certain death. Sure, you could live without stories, but it would only be half-life, a sorry existence. He told his ancestors, all those healers before him, that they would be giving the greatest gift of healing they could ever give if they would do this one thing for him.

It took them eight days to agree to try, and another ten to figure out how. Three more days and the performer from the faraway country was leaving. Drogon had to act soon on their suggestion. He wasn't sure if it would work but he had to try. Early the next morning, before the sun had risen but after the birds have begun to sing, he went to the center of the village to the story tree. This was the tree where they all met every evening for stories and at least once a week for council. It was the center of the village. As far as anyone knew, it was the reason the village was there.

The tree at the center of the village was older than memory and bigger than dreams. A dozen grown men could stand around it with arms outstretched and embrace it in a circle. Its branches stretched out 40 feet all around and were thick enough to provide shade on the hottest of days and protection on the wettest ones too. Drogon looked at it, this member of the village he'd known the longest, and told it his tale. He asked it for its permission to do what must be done to cure the people he'd never seen, would never see. He told the tree that they would sing songs about it for years in the future, to honor its sacrifice of itself. There was no answer back. He hadn't expected one, but he had tried all the same. He'd tried because to not try would have meant the guilt of what he was about to do would be on him and his descendants forever.

He assumed all must be well with the tree's silence. "In silence it went to the slaughter, a willing sacrifice, the cure for their disease." The lines of a half-forgotten prophecy came to him then and he felt better. Surely it was about this time, and this event? He felt the odd tingle of power that always happened when a prophecy came true, when *to be* became *now*.

With spirit ghosts from all of his ancestors helping, he had the tree chopped down in less than an hour, and quietly enough that none of the villagers awoke.

He had selected one log to use for the doll. It was from the heart of the tree, and was a warm sepia, the color of dry autumn leaves, the color of coffee with a hint of cream, the color of the people it had loved for so long. He had planned to carve it himself afterwards to complete the ritual, but first he had to call the spirit of the tree into it.

Right now it was like any other spirit after a trauma - floating around in the air, hovering close to its body. Car accident victims were the same. The spirit gets pushed out before it has a chance to realize that the body is no longer a safe vehicle for it. Meanwhile, it hasn't prepared itself for the journey it must now embark upon to return to the All-spirit.

Many souls think they have years before them to prepare for that mapless and solitary trip. Some are surprised at a sudden death and they linger around the body longer than they ought. There was a danger to living humans in these places - the spirit might try to take over, to evict the living soul, or to try to double-up. This led to what the villagers called "possession", and what Westerners called "mental illness". Some spirits stayed in the area of the accident for weeks afterwards, the body buried elsewhere. This meant that it was possible to cross paths with a homeless spirit without even realizing it. Perhaps this was why some people in America had started putting up roadside memorials at the site of a fatal car crash - to subtly warn others of the risk of contamination. Perhaps they knew this truth deep down, on a subconscious level.

Drogon meant to call the spirit into the wood but it was harder than he'd imagined. None of his ancestors had ever been through anything this immense, so they couldn't offer anything useful in the way of advice or warning. They were all winging it. They knew it was in their best interest, as a group, to be as careful as possible. This much energy in one place could possibly make all of them wink out of existence.

There was a reason that tree had been so big - it had held the hopes of the village for thousands of years. It had fed them with stories the same as a mother feeds her babies with milk from herself. It had sheltered them as a mother hen shelters her chicks. All of that spirit was too much to try to condense into one tiny log, but it tried. Perhaps the tree wanted to help out those nameless people who were so far away. Perhaps it trusted the village doctor, who had sat under its branches in the cool of the evening, just like his father and his father on back into the mists of time. He wouldn't bring harm, no, not him. So the tree sacrificed itself, went easily, almost willingly.

And yet it still was too much spirit to distill down into one log meant for one little doll. The energy poured in, but once the log was full (over-full, actually, in the same way you can cram more sugar into tea if you pour it in while it is hot), it spilled out, and up, and over Drogon, and in a flash of blue-violet light, embraced him, and erased him.

The sound that was created in that moment was like the sound of a waterfall swollen by spring rains, or that of a thousand bees swarming to find a new nest. It was sudden and sure and scary, like a lion before it charges upon a hyena foolish enough to prey upon his family. It was then that the rest of the villagers awoke to discover the remains of Drogon next to the felled tree. They ran to find Drogon's son, knowing that he would now be able to explain what happened. The only reason they knew it was Drogon was from his clothes and the beaded jewelry he always wore. His body had been reduced to ash.

Drogon's son, only seven years old but now the village doctor, took it upon himself to complete the doll. It had to be done. Otherwise, the death of the tree would have been in vain. He also had to atone for the actions of his father, as well as the ancestors who had agreed to this disastrous plan.

Out of a sense of guilt, the lady from the faraway land offered the villagers ten times the amount of money for the doll than she had originally agreed to. They wanted nothing - no money, no school, no hospital. Nothing could repay them for the loss of their tree. To accept payment would be to cheapen its sacrifice. They gave her the completed doll, hoping to never see it or her ever again.

The lady went on to become famous for her ventriloquist act, retiring earlier than she'd hoped. Her fans were amazed at how much better she had become. The skits were sharper, wittier, if a little edgy these days. They marveled at how adept she had become at throwing her voice without apparently having her mouth open.

She kept the doll with her all the time to keep her secret. She lived alone for the same reason. When she had first returned from her trip, she was living in an apartment, but soon made enough to move to a large home, far away from people. This was good, because otherwise they would have heard the wooden dolly arguing with her owner.

It all came to an end one humid summer night when the home went up in flames, reducing both the lady and the doll to ashes. Arson investigators scoured the ruined property shaking their heads. They agreed that the fire looked like it was set on purpose by the doll, but since this made no sense, they quietly agreed to officially state that the performer had dropped a cigarette while smoking in bed.

(Originally posted 5-17-17)

The Pickers

Charlie and Rex played together every day, but not like most. Little boys and mutts were usually fast friends, playing tag or chase or tug-of-war. But not these two. Charlie's dad got him the banjo the same time he got him the dog. Sure, the banjo wasn't child-sized. Mr. Jason Reinsch didn't have enough money to buy something that Charlie would outgrow soon enough. So he got him an adult one at a used musical instrument store. He got Rex from what he liked to think of as the used dog store.

There were a lot of choices of instruments there - all castoffs from the hundreds of hopeful people who came to their city every month, trying to become the next big star. Trouble was that very few of them had much talent, and even fewer had the discipline to make anything of it. There were instruments in there that had been bought and sold a half-dozen times, all at a small profit to Zeke, the owner. He didn't want to charge too much, but he had bills to pay the same as anybody else, so he did what he had to do.

Charlie had never met Zeke or anybody else in the music business before then, but things changed. Once word got out about his act with Rex, he met nearly everybody who was attached to the music business. It seemed like that was most of the town in one way or another. If they weren't actual musicians, they were songwriters, or producers, or agents, or roadies, or fans. Everybody wanted to see Charlie and Rex play. It hadn't been like that at the beginning.

Charlie first learned bluegrass songs because that was what his dad knew. Why try to pretend to be an expert in something you know nothing about? That was a sure path to ruin. No, best to stick with what you know and build up on that. It wasn't long before he was picking out a passable rendition of such classics as "Muddy Road to Ducktown" and "Dream of a Miner's Child". The latter was especially well-received because he hammed it up with a little soot on his cheeks to play the part.

He wasn't a miner's child, of course, but there were some similarities. His dad, Jason, dug out precious gems in a way - he was a picker. He never could see a way to having a full-time job, even when he had a wife and five children to support. He was too independent for that. He wasn't one to submit to a boss, especially one who thought he could tell Jason how to complete the task he'd never even personally tried. Why did so many businesses think it was a good idea to have a supervisor who was a stranger to the task at hand? He had bosses try to tell him what to do in his first couple of jobs, thought better of it, and decided that as soon as he could, he'd never have anybody above him

Times were sure lean when he was married with children. All those mouths to feed and backs to clothe! A few years ago his wife and the children had wanted a dog and he put his foot down. He couldn't see clear to how that would even be possible. It was hard enough making do with the earnings he made from up-selling his finds to antique malls and consignment shops. Did they expect him to rent a booth at the flea market as well to pay for the dog's needs? That was too much like what he was trying to avoid.

Spring left him and took four of the kids one afternoon to her sister's house and never came back. Jason had taken Charlie to the hardware store to get some chicken wire. He had the idea that raising his own chickens would save a lot of money in the long run, what with not having to buy eggs or meat ever again. He didn't know anything about raising chickens, but he hadn't known anything about raising children either and hadn't done too bad. Or so he thought.

Spring was fed up with his get-rich-quick schemes that always turned out to be get-poor-slow ones instead. He never gave up, which in some situations is an admirable trait. But sometimes it is good to know when the time has come to move on and let go.

Like now. Spring was through with his promises that never work fulfilled, his dreams that seemed more like nightmares. Without even leaving a note, she left. Sure, she missed Charlie, but four other children were plenty enough to keep up with, and Charlie had been Jason's favorite after all.

Jason noticed the quiet first when he got home. It seemed so peaceful. He couldn't ever remember a time when the house didn't have at least some noise from some child banging on something or his wife complaining about something else. He then noticed why it was so quiet. It was just him and Charlie there. This was unusual for his wife to leave without saying anything.

He was so grateful for the quiet that he decided to take a nap right then and there in the middle of the day. The last time he'd done that he'd been in kindergarten. It was just as delicious and just as needed now. Jason decided he'd take a nap every day from now on out. This was yet another reason not having to work for "the man" was a great idea. He could nap anytime he felt like it.

What did Spring know anyway? Always whining at him about how he needed to grow up and be a man. What did she know about being a man? She wasn't one. She had no idea how hard it was to carry all this responsibility. It was a miracle he hadn't snapped like some guys did and started killing people. Mass murder and road rage came from the same root after all - unexpressed anger. Jason figured it was best to not get angry in the first place, so he avoided everything and everyone that made him angry. Well, except for his wife of course. He meant it when he said his vows. Divorce wasn't an option in his mind, no matter how hard it got.

Things were easier now that it was just him and Charlie. Less to keep up with. Sure it was harder without Mary to keep on top of the household things, but he could manage. He did before he met her, didn't he? If the dishes didn't get washed for a week, who would it bother? It seemed a waste of time to have to do it so often. She was always nagging about every little thing. He was better off with her elsewhere. He kind of missed the other kids, but Charlie really was his favorite. This meant they got to spend more time together, undisturbed by everyone else.

Of course, with Mary gone, he had to keep up with Charlie all the time now. He was too young to leave alone at home, like you could with a dog. That was how Jason came up with the idea of getting a dog and teaching them both to sing for their supper. This way he could set them outside on the curb to perform while he was doing the grocery shopping. The home farm hadn't yet taken off like he thought, so there were still carrots and broccoli and potatoes to buy. Even when his crop did come in, he'd still have to go get milk and fruit. No way was he going to raise a cow or fruit trees. Too much work, and Jason was all about putting in the least amount of effort. If he could get someone else to do the work for him, all the better.

Charlie took to the banjo like a duck takes to water, and Rex was happy to howl along. Jason hadn't figured having him as part of the act but it was sure funny to see him crooning in more or less in the right pitch. His timing was a little off but practice would fix that. Plus, he soon realized, people weren't as likely to call the authorities when they saw them together. It was as if they thought the dog was a suitable guardian for Charlie, little as he was. Alone, they thought he was abandoned or had wandered off and tended to call the police to check up on things. But the dog there? That was okay somehow and they let them be.

Jason was through trying to figure out why people thought and acted the way they did, so as long as things worked out in his favor. His wife leaving him was certainly working out, better than he'd ever expected. Not like he'd even imagine she'd leave. But he certainly wasn't one to pass up a good thing that came his way. That was part of the picker mentality, after all.

(Originally posted 7-26-17)

About the "Adopt a relative" series -

This is what started it all. I think. How do you know when you have begun something that you stayed with? I didn't plan on this being a thing. I didn't know I'd be publishing this. I didn't know then that I'd know how. But here I am with my seventh book, a work of fiction.

Some of these pictures are digital copies from my blog. The original pictures are lost somewhere in my journals, or I never owned them. There is an antique mall in Boone, North Carolina on King Street. One of the booths has a box entitled "Adopt a Relative". It is filled with black and white pictures of anonymous people, taken from old family photo albums. Were they donated? Were they found in yard sales, or flea markets, or trash bins? I don't know. Does it matter?

I was struck by how many pictures there were of babies sitting on lawns. Not held by anyone. Seemingly alone. Who were these children? Why were they unattended? Maybe they were outside because flash photography hadn't been invented yet and sunlight was the best light available. But why wasn't anyone holding them? Was the child more important than the parent?

I'd never tried my hand at writing fiction, but these snapshots needed answers to these questions, and there was no other way to get them. Closure is one of the biggest drives in humans. We have to know what, and why, and who, and when, and how. It is why reporters and detectives do what they do. The answers I needed couldn't be found on the Internet, but they could be found in my head, it turned out. I hope you enjoy them. And if you know who these people are, please let me know.

The bramble-bush baby

He found the feral child on Wednesday, under the bramble-bush. Hank had meant to cut that bush down six weeks ago, after that toad-strangling thunderstorm. Said it would loosen up the roots, make it easier to get out, to do it then. He forgot, or put it by, maybe hoping Ellie wouldn't remember that she'd asked.

She hadn't. That was all he heard about. She left him notes. She asked him after he came home from work. She suggested that today looked like a good day. It started off once a week that she'd remind him, but then it was twice a week. Then it was more. At 8 that Wednesday morning he finally got tired of her reminding him, so out he went, hoe in hand.

He thought he saw something odd the moment he stepped out the back door. A bit of laundry blown over from Mrs. Whipple's house? A piece of paper from a torn-open bag of trash? The wind was forever driving things into their yard.

The wind drove a baby into their yard this time.

The moment Hank saw it, dark-eyed and brooding, with a narrow-eyed stare that thinly hid years of malice and hate behind them, he knew this was a baby in size only. Knew right then and there it wasn't human, neither. He ran back inside, more afraid of that child than of the ribbing he'd get from Ellie at bein' a'feared of anything. First off he'd have to explain how he wasn't shirking the bramble-bush chore. That alone was enough to make him think twice about going all the way back inside.

He stood a bit in the mud-room, on that peeling linoleum floor, trying to decide. He'd known Ellie for 18 years. He just met that baby, if a baby it really was. He decided he was better off going back outside. He knew how Ellie got when she was angry. He'd take his chances with the baby.

(Originally posted 10-22-15)

Betsy Nelson

Hilda in the snow

Hilda was shivering. Cousin Tom insisted on taking her picture. She protested, mildly. "You can't take my picture - it can't even be given away." She mentioned an old tale she'd read in one of the many folktale books she'd found to while away the time in these cold winter months. "Some cultures say that taking pictures takes the soul, others say that it is making a graven image, and that's a sin." When pressed, she couldn't remember what culture said it, or if there were more than one that had this belief.

Tom was having none of it. "The sooner you let me take this picture, the sooner you can be inside," he retorted. That was enough for Hilda. 10 feet away, stock still, she stood. The moment she heard the metallic click of the shutter release she was free. She trudged back inside, her duty done.

He said he was going to take a picture of all his relatives, save them up in an album. He'd include labels too, with history, birthdate, the lot. Maybe even accomplishments. She thought he should include that she'd won first prize in typing at the local career college.

Typing wasn't her thing. It was her parent's idea. She'd always wanted to be a cellist for some big symphony in some city - anywhere away from here. The sound of the cello reached down to her bones with its warmth, all golden-honey smooth. Her parents thought this was poppycock, wasteful, a dreamer's fantasy, and told her often, even if she hadn't brought the subject up that week. She was going to be a secretary and that was that. They paid good money for those typing classes and weren't going to have her waste it with some fool idea of playing an instrument they'd never even seen in real life.

They decided they had to do something to prepare for her future. That was the reason for the classes. They had no ambitions she'd ever get married, so she'd have to support herself after they'd passed on.

They would never say she was ugly, at least not out loud. Homely. Plain, even. "She has a great personality," they'd chirp to new acquaintances, in the off chance they might have a son in a similar predicament. Even if a date did come of it, there never was a second one. The boys all said "You think too much," and that was that. The guy didn't want her, and she didn't want him.

"Like thinking too much is a bad thing," she'd say to herself. She wasn't one to dumb herself down to their level. They'd either have to rise to hers or she do without a man in her life. That suited her just fine.

Meanwhile, she was cold, and her party shoes were now ruined from that snow.

(Originally posted 10-23-15)

Tilly and the lawn

It was a big yard, and somebody had to mow it. 82° in the shade, and there wasn't much of that to be had, but the grass still needed mowing.

Tilly was pleased with herself. All 7 acres in one day! Maurice said it couldn't be done, but she did it. All week long he doubted her and it only egged her on. It was years later before she suspected that was his plan - to fire her up to do it by saying she couldn't.

He was forever getting out of doing things one way or another. He thought he was so clever, but she was the real winner. He spent his whole life making others do everything for him and had never learned how to do anything for himself. Now he was a manager at a forgotten branch office of a small appliance outlet. Upper management had been fooled for years, thinking he did all the work.

When employee after employee quit, the house of cards tumbled down. They'd held it together for a very long time, but there was only so much they could take, watching him get the praise, the bonuses, the requests for motivational speeches. They couldn't get why nobody else could see through his lies. Finally they left, one by one, and he was left by himself to run the shop. He didn't even know how to run the cash register. It took the corporate office a week to suspect something was wrong. It took them a month to find an out-of-the-way office where he couldn't do the company a lot of damage.

They couldn't fire him, no, that wouldn't do. Nobody really knew why. It wasn't like he had tenure, not officially. This wasn't a college after all. Plenty of half-rate incompetents had slid under the wire in that field. He was likable, in an odd kind of way. Perhaps that was how he could cajole everyone - employees, family, neighbors, into doing things for him.

He wasn't pushy in an obvious kind of way. He just knew how to put a little pressure here and a little finesse there and before you knew it you'd agree to give up your one day off to work his shift. Somehow, at the time, you forgot you had plans you made weeks ago with friends you'd not seen since September. Somehow, it took several hours into your shift - his shift - to remember, and get angry and even a little resentful.

He was far away by then, and maybe that was part of his magic. The closer he was to you, the more you couldn't resist, the more you couldn't say no. Even 30-some-odd feet away at the other end of the building, his influence could still be felt. When he was at home he didn't have the same power over them. But he sure had it over his wife.

Tilly made less than Maurice, always had. She was fine with that, because she had something he'd never have, something more than money. She had respect. She was respected by her coworkers and her family - people who had to be around her. Her friends didn't just respect her - they adored her. They were drawn to her charm like a child is drawn to fireflies. They all did what she asked joyfully because she rarely asked - asked only when absolutely necessary, and even then she always said "You can say no". They never did.

Doing for her was like doing for a saint. You felt better after doing it, whatever the task.

Years later Tilly saw the picture of her standing on the front porch and laughed. If she'd only known just a few years later there'd be gas powered motors to speed things up. Just a few years later and there'd be tennis shoes, not loafers, for better grip. Just a few years later and she could have worn a T-shirt and shorts to do this chore, free to choose to wear a dress rather then it be the only option. All these advancements made her mowing accomplishment at the time all the more impressive because she did it without them.

She'd always thought that handicaps were advantages in disguise. They made you work harder, not take anything for granted. They handicapped the athletes who were stronger, didn't they? Or was it horses? Something about making it a fair match. So being handicapped meant something good to her, meant that she secretly was better, stronger, more capable. Like she had secret powers and had to figure out what they were, hidden under that handicap. She always said that the more you focus on what you don't have, the more you miss what you do.

Maurice was her handicap, so he was also her blessing. Because of him she learned how not to treat others. He gave her so many examples of how not to act that she had a clear road in front of her showing her the way. It was like he'd gone through the test book of life and crossed out all the wrong answers, leaving her with all the right ones. It was an odd way of learning but it was learning nonetheless. It took her years to understand the gift that he given her by teaching her backwards.

(Originally posted 10-30-15)

Waiting

It wasn't long now. They said they were coming back. Only problem was that they didn't say when. So every day at 3 o'clock she went outside and looked towards the horizon, wearing her best clothes. Every day she stood in the same spot near the plain gray house, waiting.

The first day she waited three whole hours. She stood most of that time, wanting to appear as eager and ready on the outside and she felt inside. It wouldn't do to look ungrateful for the gift they promised. Wouldn't do to seem indifferent or casual about such an opportunity. After a while her legs got tired, so she sat on the Adirondack chair even though it was almost as uncomfortable as sitting on a pew. She had plenty enough of that kind of sitting. That was why she was so eager to go.

Still she waited, and still they made her wait. Maybe they forgot? Maybe this was a test? Maybe they reckoned time differently than earthlings did?

She kept the Visitation secret from Paw and her brother. They'd wonder about her if she told. If Maw was still around she'd have been sent down the river to the State Hospital, like how all the other rejects and misfits were sent, those who heard voices and saw people who weren't there to everybody else. They were trash as far as the village saw it, so down they went, along with the barges of other broken and forgotten things. They took the Bible seriously when it said "You must purge the evil from among you." Too bad their definition of evil was very wide.

She was safe now in part because she was female. The men-folk didn't want to have to do all the cleaning and cooking. So even if they suspected something was amiss they'd be reluctant to send her away because they'd have to take up her chores. It didn't mean they wouldn't send her anyway, because harboring a defective was grounds for being sent downriver along with. Better to sacrifice your child or your spouse than to go yourself. A lifetime of building up the homestead wasted, and for nothing.

So still she waited, every day hopeful that would be the day. This was the 438th day, a Wednesday. She had waiting down to an art, if not a science, by now. She'd learned to finish her chores an hour before, and then to change into Church clothes at least 20 minutes before the time to go outside. Once, early on, she'd left it too late and didn't have time to put her shoes on. Barefoot was better than left behind, so out into the prickly grass she went. She'd learned to do better from then on.

It took a while for Paw to get used to her going outside and waiting every day. At first she took a book with her as a cover, saying it was better for her eyes to read in natural light. He didn't argue with that, thinking maybe it would save money on glasses in the future. He wasn't keen on spending money at all, but much less so when it came to his daughter. He had no use for her. She wasn't going to inherit the farm or the family name, so why bother? She was just another mouth to feed, and after that a dowry to pay. Made no sense to have to pay a man to marry his daughter, but that was how it was and no changing it.

Yet another reason to get away. She had no plans on marrying, of having to have some other man tell her what to do and when to do it. The ones who came promised her she'd never have to get married because they didn't marry where they came from. Didn't have a need of it. There, people were able to take care of themselves once they were grown up. They didn't need to live with another person like a child would. They had partnerships, sure, but making legal commitments to each other just complicated things. They had understandings and agreements, without the need for a piece of paper or a judicial system. To complicate something as sacred as a partnership of any sort with the law meant that you were planning on trouble. If you didn't think it was going to work out, it was best not to make a partnership at all.

They promised her a lot, more than she believed or could imagine. But everything else they had promised and delivered on was truer than true, and lasting. She knew they were good to their word because they'd already shown her miracles. They'd given her a locket that told the future. It showed her some of what would happen the next day, choices she could make to change things. Just small things, but small was better than nothing. All she had to do was open it and she'd have an edge on everyone else. She kept it closed most of the time, but it was good to know she had this small advantage, this small proof that the Visitation was real. She had a hard time believing it after so many days of waiting.

She kept the locket they gave her secret, under her clothes. Wouldn't do to have it visible, or lost, wouldn't do to leave it in her jewelry box, to be stolen like every other special thing she'd ever had. Her brother felt no guilt about coming in her room, going through her drawers and treasure boxes, taking whatever caught his fancy. He needed money for a new baseball mitt or the latest style of shoes, he'd take it from her, no asking.

It took her a while to realize that things went missing. At first she thought maybe she'd spent some of it and hadn't remembered to write it down. After a few weeks of money going missing, she had her suspicions and started keeping the tally in a separate place. When she showed the proof to Paw he just shrugged, saying "Boys will be boys", like stealing was normal for boys. The part he didn't say was that it meant being robbed was normal for girls. Too bad that being family meant nothing. No protection from thievery, of having your possessions, yourself, violated.

They promised that there she'd never have to worry about anything being stolen, not ever again. Never have to worry about being sick neither. Her personal safety was assured, and life would not only be better, but longer. Not immortal, mind you. Plenty others had promised that and couldn't deliver. The trick there was simply living longer than anyone around you. They died, thinking you were immortal, when really you were just slowed down. There's a reason hummingbirds have such short lives and turtles such long ones. Slow the heart rate down, slow the breathing down, and it seems like you are on the fast track to a long life.

She didn't have to worry about taking medicine to slow her heart rate where she was going. They'd take out her human heart entirely, replace it with one they'd grown just for her, a better one. That would be the first thing replaced. They'd taken samples to grow a whole set of organs for her with plenty of cells to spare if something wore out sooner than expected. Lungs, pancreas, eyes, the lot. Grown as needed, one by one.

When they first started they had cloned people. Not just the organs, but the whole kit and caboodle, stem to stern. Seemed a good idea until it came time to harvest and turned out the clones weren't too willing to part with their parts. Whole new kinds of laws were developed then, saying these were now people, with rights, and not a collection of replacement bits to be switched out like a used fan belt or alternator you'd pick up at the local auto yard. Once they figured out how to grow the organs separately there weren't any problems. A liver can't complain with no mouth to talk with.

They promised painless surgery too. The organs would be exchanged by a form of highly localized teleportation. Beam the old one out and the new one in at the same time, like a kind of cross-fade, like in music. Hurt less than getting a shot, they said.

She was still waiting. Maybe she'd stay a little longer outside today, just in case, what with the time change and all.

(Originally posted 11-6-15)

Babies on the Lawn

Maynardsville awoke to a crop of babies on their lawns last Wednesday. The first to notice was Mr. Eugene Tomlinson. He was up earlier than usual because of his lumbago. The familiar dull ache had kept him tossing half of the night, so when he heard the first sounds of the birds that morning, he decided to get up rather than fight through that racket as well. Eugene opened his front door to see if the newspaper was there and found a baby instead.

It was sitting in a chair, pretty as you please, smiling at him. He noticed it was wearing a bonnet and a dress so he guessed it was a girl, but you never can tell with babies. Just like with the very old, the very young are all genderless, with the only clues being the accessories.

"Well, Eugene, what do we do now?" he said to himself. He'd been in the habit of talking to himself in the first person plural since his wife died three years ago after the flood. He felt less lonely this way and often got the right answer too. It was as if she was still with him, still advising him. He imagined he could still hear her voice. Perhaps this was a side effect of being married for over 40 years. Well over half his life it was.

Right now she was saying "Well, pick her up and take her inside. You don't want her to catch cold."

"But Emma, I don't have any food for her. What'll I feed her?"

"Don't you worry about that." She replied in his heart. "We aren't planning on keeping her. She isn't a stray kitten. Call the police. Surely somebody's missing a baby."

Always reasonable, his Emma. These days he only really missed her around supper time.

Frozen dinners were a far cry from her scratch-made meals. They fed the body, but not the soul.

Now, how to pick this thing up? It'd been a long time since he'd had to handle a baby, and there'd been no grandchildren to practice on. Eugene wasn't sure whether to approach it like a landmine or a piece of Wedgewood. Will it blow up? Will it break? Thankfully the baby didn't wiggle much, even put its arms up to be held. Eugene noticed she smelled good. This is a bonus with babies. Makes it easier to be with them in an enclosed space like the efficiency apartment he had. The whole block was full of them, and they were full of old people. This couldn't be a neighbor's child. Maybe a grandchild? Maybe a foster? Even though he'd lived here two years he still didn't know his neighbors well enough to know details like this. Heck, who was he kidding? He didn't even know their names.

Eugene put the baby on the rug in the living room. She didn't look capable of staying in one place on the couch. He couldn't remember how old babies were before they stopped falling out of bed. Couches were worse - much narrower. Better not take any chances.

After getting this mystery child settled, he reached for the phone near the television and called the police. He was on hold for quite a while, long enough to start humming along to the hold music. When he was finally connected and was able to explain his predicament he was told that a dozen other found babies had been discovered and reported in the meantime. The only problem was that nobody else had reported any of them lost.

Over the course of the day, more and more babies appeared on the lawns all over the city. It wasn't that they materialized. They didn't fade in, like Kirk and Dr. McCoy beaming down to a planet. They were just there, sitting on the lawn. Plenty of people walked out first thing to go to work, or walk the dog, or buy a breakfast sandwich at the corner shop and there wouldn't be a baby. But when they returned, one would be there.

Not everybody was visited by these tiny guests. There didn't seem to be a pattern to who got one and who didn't. There did seem to be a few things that were common among them, though. They were all white, and they were all smiling. All were too young to explain where they came from and who their parents were. But all of them were unflappable. It was eerie how calm and contented these babies were. It made a difficult situation a little more tolerable.

Some appeared along with chairs. Most had clothes. Some didn't. Fortunately those appeared in the afternoon after the morning chill had burned off.

All told, 387 babies showed up that Wednesday. Some went to foster homes. Some went to the hospital. One enterprising person set up a nanny service in the disused hotel at the eastern edge of town.

Some childless couples felt these babies were answers to their prayers. Others remembered why they never had children in the first place. Plenty of well-meaning folks had told them they'd change their minds when they had one, but it wasn't true. Even though these babies were cheery, they were still babies, which meant they needed constant attention. Even going to the bathroom had to be done quickly or else something got destroyed by the babies - either through breakage or bodily fluids. In this they were a lot like puppies, but unlike puppies they couldn't be left alone at home when it was time to go to work. There are laws about that.

A lot of people had to stay home that Thursday because of that. Those were the ones who weren't lucky enough to have been in the first wave of babies sprouting up on the lawn, like mushrooms overnight. Weren't lucky enough to have handed them off to the authorities - any authority - anybody who would take them off their hands. Some older folks tried to contact the orphanage, forgetting that there wasn't one, hadn't been one for many a year. Spare children - those without parents who were living, or those with parents who weren't capable of being a parent (due to disease or disinclination) were shuttled off to the foster care system instead of the orphanage these days. The result was that they were just as lost and broken as if they'd been institutionalized, but it took longer to notice since they weren't housed under the same roof.

A town meeting was called for that Friday afternoon, and everybody came, babies in tow. There weren't enough babysitters to go around. "Somebody has to do something!" Myra Tuttle exclaimed, baby on hip. "It's the Russians! They've done this to us!" yelled Bob Flanders, a child crawling in and out between his feet as he sat.

The mayor agreed something had to be done and tried to squash the idea of a conspiracy from the Russians, or aliens as Thomas Wilson had suggested. She said it didn't matter who or why but that, and that was where they were. The hotel on the east end was the best option for emergency use as the enterprising nanny had proven, so the city summarily took it over without paying for it, said something about "eminent domain" and pressed all city employees who could be spared into service as full-time babysitters.

After a week, a total of 2,347 babies had appeared. Then it stopped, just as suddenly as it started, and the town breathed a collective sigh of relief. Now they knew what their new normal was. They could make a plan. They waited a month to be sure. You can handle anything unusual as long as it stays the same for a while.

(Originally posted 12-14-15)

Betsy Nelson

AFTERWORD

Once I had a friend who saw me making a rosary. She knew I liked science fiction, and we were in a medieval reenactment group together. We had talked about many esoteric things. She described our way of knowing as "weird".

She looked at me making this very religious object and said "How can you make that? Aren't you 'weird'?" I paused for a moment. Outing yourself as a follower of Jesus can alienate you to a lot of people. But it is important to be honest and share what you know to be good.

I said to her "Jesus was weird. He walked on water. He fed 5000 people with just a loaf of bread and a few fish. He challenged the religious authorities and told them that what they were doing was wrong. He healed people for free. He raised people from the dead. He told people to love their enemies and forgive them for everything. Nobody is weirder than Jesus." From that point onward she looked at Jesus differently, and she and her family started attending church.

I would be remiss if I didn't tell you who my greatest influence in life is. It's Jesus. These aren't Christian stories, however. The stories are odd. They make you think. But Jesus is odd too. And Jesus wants you to think and to pay close attention to what God expects of you, instead of what the world expects.

Anything in here that makes you wonder about creation, that gives you hope – that is from God. Anything in here that is just plain strange – that is from me. I hope these stories help you to see the world with new eyes.

Alphabetical index of titles

Strange books

Here is a short list of books from other authors that you might like to explore. Some are intended for children, but adults will also find them amazing. Some are non-fiction. Some don't have any words at all. If you can't find them at your local library, ask them to get them for you through Inter-Library Loan (ILL).

Alexander, Christopher W. *A Pattern Language: Towns, Buildings, Construction*

Anderson, Walter Inglis. *The Horn Island Logs of Walter Inglis Anderson*

Arndt, Ingo. *Animal Architecture*

Bantock, Nick. *Griffin and Sabine* (series)

Barklem, Jill. *The Secret Staircase*

Becker, Aaron. *Journey* (series)

Bender, Tom. *Silence Song and Shadows: Our Need for the Sacred in Our Surroundings*

Berry, Jill K. *Map Art Lab: 52 Exciting Art Explorations in Mapmaking, Imagination, and Travel*

Brown, Patricia D. *Paths to Prayer: Finding Your Own Way to the Presence of God*

Brown, Peter.   *Mr. Tiger Goes Wild*

Cameron, Julia.   *The Complete Artist's Way: Creativity as a Spiritual Practice*

Castaneda, Carlos.   *The Teachings of Don Juan: A Yaqui Way of Knowledge*

Chapin, Ross.   *Pocket Neighborhoods: Creating Small-Scale Community in a Large-Scale World*

Cloud, Henry.   *Boundaries: When to Say Yes, How to Say No to Take Control of Your Life*

Collins, Ross.   *Doodleday*

Dass, Ram.   *Be Here Now*

Dick, Philip K.   *Do Androids Dream of Electric Sheep?*

Egan, Tim.   *The Pink Refrigerator*

Elgin, Suzette Haden.   *Star-Anchored, Star-Angered*

Ewing, Al.   *I, Zombie*

Foster, Alan Dean.   *Cyber Way*

Gaiman, Neil.   *The Sandman* (series)

Goldsworthy, Andy.   *Andy Goldsworthy: A Collaboration with Nature*

Hall, Michael.   *Red: A Crayon's Story*

Hallendy, Norman.   *Inuksuit: Silent Messengers of the Arctic*

Hoff, Benjamin.   *The Tao of Pooh*

Kalman, Maira.   *The Principles of Uncertainty*

Lawhead, Stephen R.   *The Skin Map* (Bright Empires series

L'Engle, Madeleine.   *A Wrinkle in Time* (series)

Lehman, Barbara.   *Museum Trip*

Martin, Bruce T.   *Look Close, See Far: A Cultural Portrait of the Maya*

Miles, Sara.   *Take This Bread: A Radical Conversion*

Neeper, Cary.   *A Place Beyond Man: The Archives of Varok*

Pohl, Frederik.   *A Plague of Pythons*

Pratchett, Terry.   *Small Gods* (Discworld series)

Rex, Adam.   *Frankenstein Makes a Sandwich*

Roach, Mary.   *Stiff: The Curious Lives of Human Cadavers*

Rumi, Jalaluddin.   *The Soul of Rumi: A New Collection of Ecstatic Poems*

Seuss, Dr.   *Did I Ever Tell You How Lucky You Are?*

Smith, Keri.   *Wreck This Journal*

Snodgrass, Melinda M.   *The Tears of the Singers*

Spangler, Ann.   *Sitting at the Feet of Rabbi Jesus: How the Jewishness of Jesus Can Transform Your Faith*

Swift, Vivian.   *When Wanderers Cease to Roam: A Traveler's Journal of Staying Put*

Tan, Shaun.   *The Arrival*

Tolkien, J.R.R.   *The Hobbit*

Wiesner, David.   *Tuesday*

Willems, Mo.   *You Can Never Find a Rickshaw When It Monsoons: The World on One Cartoon a Day*

ABOUT THE AUTHOR

Betsy Nelson seeks to build bridges between people. She is a facilitator in the Circle process of nonviolent conflict resolution, as well as a trained Remo HealthRhythms facilitator. She has also successfully completed a clinical experiential course in the art and practice of pastoral care. She is a certified Reiki practitioner and also co-facilitates a regular Centering Prayer group.

She has volunteered in the Metro Nashville public schools since 2011, primarily tutoring kindergartners from other countries or who have learning disabilities. She has taught bimonthly prayer bracelet workshops since 2015, as well as facilitated many art classes for adults. She also enjoys sharing mail art with pen pals all over the world.

Her writing has appeared in the Huffington Post. She is a contributor to an online inspirational magazine called My Spiritual Breakfast, as well as the online communities known as Daily Inspiration and The Wander Society. She obtained her Bachelor's degree in English, with a concentration in writing, from the University of Tennessee at Chattanooga.

She is married and lives near Nashville, TN. She has worked for the public library system since 2000, where she is fortunate to get to serve and learn from people from all walks of life.

You can follow her journey online at betsybeadhead.com

Other books by this author -

Free Range Faith, Dec 11, 2014 (essays on following Jesus and not Christianity)

Fortunate Stamps, Jan 17, 2015 (collage using stamps and fortune cookie messages)

The Condensed Gospel, Dec 19, 2015 (the Gospel, as one story, in order, with no repetition)

Travel by Stamps, Dec 27, 2015 (a children's story using vintage stamps for the illustrations)

Some for the Road: Meditations and milestones on the road of recovery, Apr 22, 2017 (Daily meditations on recovery.)

Images of God (in color), Jun 21, 2017 (inspirational poetry and pictures, in full color)

Images of God (in black and white), Jun 23, 2017 (inspirational poetry and pictures, in the more affordable format of black and white)

75035543R00131

Made in the USA
Lexington, KY
17 December 2017